DAWN LEE MCKENNA'S

# LOW TIDE

## A *FORGOTTEN COAST* SUSPENSE NOVEL:
## BOOK ONE

2015

A SWEET TEA PRESS PUBLICATION

First published in the United States by Sweet Tea Press

Edited by Tammi Labrecque
larksandkatydids.com

Cover by Shayne Rutherford
darkmoongraphics.com

Interior Design by Colleen Sheehan
wdrbookdesign.com

*Low Tide* is a work of fiction. All incidents and dialogue, and all characters, are products of the author's imagination. Any similarities to any person, living or dead, is merely coincidental.

*For Mom*

*Who generously waters late bloomers*

# CHAPTER

# ONE

The seagulls bounced around him, lighting just long enough to snatch up the pieces of bread, then hovering in the air, wings whipping, to wait for more.

Gulls were mercenary and self-absorbed, but he liked them. They were honest about their selfishness, unafraid of disapproval. At the same time, they were beautiful and graceful and they were the sight and sound of home.

He'd spent his entire life in Apalachicola and on St. George Island, just a few miles from the coast across the causeway. To his mind, it was one of the few places left that actually felt like Florida, with its century-old brick and clapboard shops and houses, the marina filled with shrimp and oyster boats and people who couldn't care less about Disney World.

Every time he'd left the Panhandle, for college or just to escape, he'd always felt slightly lost. Cities and nightlife and people with unfamiliar last names quickly lost their luster. Whenever he'd arrived home, after a few weeks or a few years, he'd felt his lungs open up to the salt and the heat and he'd known that he hadn't really breathed since he'd left.

Always, he came here first, to this virtually undisturbed, un-blemished part of the island that was now a state park. Here, he could be the only sign of humanity among the white dunes and the sea grasses and the gulls and crabs that lived among them. Looking out to the ocean, he felt at once humbled and comforted by his own unimportance.

This was his sanctuary, his place of respite and refreshment. Here, there were no problems; there were no decisions or respon-sibilities or agendas. He could come here and empty his mind. He could fill his lungs with great, hungry breaths of salty air and be renewed, then go back to the mainland stronger, calmer, more ready to deal with his life and the people in it.

A gust of early-summer wind snatched at the plastic bag of bread, winding it around his wrist and causing the hovering seagulls to reverse themselves in the air, putting a few feet of dis-tance between them and him. He unwrapped the almost-empty bag from his wrist and the gulls moved back in as he tossed out a few more pieces of crust.

He often felt like this group of gulls was the same group that he'd fed every time he'd ever come, the same birds he'd fed when he was ten or twenty. He felt like they remembered him, knew him and waited here for him when he was gone. They were his friends, really, or so he felt. They made him happy, with their flapping and grabbing and screeching.

He tossed out the last of the bread and the gulls landed in per-fect synchronicity, like one being. He stuffed the bag in the left pocket of his khakis so that it wouldn't be a danger to the sea creatures, then pulled the gun from his waistband and slowly sat down on the sand.

A few minutes later, the explosion from the gun sent the gulls screeching into the air, then gradually, tentatively, they all came back to the sand. The ones with blood splattered on their gray and white bodies seemed especially agitated, even for seagulls.

Maggie Redmond pulled the coverlet over her head as her cell phone bleated from the nightstand.

"No," she grumbled from under the covers, but the bleating continued and the coverlet did little to block the late morning sun.

She snaked a hand out from under the covers and pulled the cell phone in, thumbing the *answer* button.

"I just went to bed. If this isn't life threatening, hang up."

"No," she heard Wyatt Hamilton rumble back. Wyatt was the Sheriff of Franklin County and her boss. "I need you to come over to St. George Island. Got a guy that shot himself on the beach."

"So? How badly is he hurt?"

"I don't know how bad it hurt, but it sure as hell killed him," Wyatt said.

"Ugh. Did you tell him it was my first day off in two weeks?"

"I mentioned it," he answered. "We're at the first pull-off before you get to the state park."

"Do I have time to take a shower?"

"Well, he's awfully close to the shoreline and the seagulls keep making off with chunks of his childhood memories, but you're the investigator, so it's your call."

"Alright. Stop it," Maggie said, throwing her legs over the side of the bed. "Give me thirty minutes."

"Okay," Wyatt told her. "I know you're gonna stop at Café Con Leche. Bring me one."

"Do you have an ID?" Maggie asked as she stood up and pinched at her eyes.

"Yeah. Gregory Boudreaux," Wyatt answered, then hung up.

It took Maggie a minute to put the phone down on the bed. It also took her a minute to remember to exhale. She walked into the bathroom and turned on the cold water tap. She splashed a couple of handfuls of water onto her face and stood and looked in the mirror.

Then she leaned over and threw up into the toilet.

Getting to St. George Island by car involved taking US 98, a five-mile or so causeway across East Bay to Eastpoint, then taking 300, another causeway that seemed to run four miles out into the Gulf of Mexico and stop, but which actually ended at St. George.

There were days like today, when cloud cover was low, that Maggie got the impression she was driving out to some distant point on the horizon, leaving the mainland behind her for good. Off to her left was Dog Island, a state preserve with more egrets and gators than people. To her right was Cape St. George Island State Preserve, just a few yards of ocean from St. George itself.

Maggie rolled her window down and breathed deeply of the thick, salty air. She was driving straight into the morning sun and it scalded her eyes, already dry and tender from lack of sleep. She'd left her sunglasses at home, so she blinked several times to soothe her eyes and pulled the visor down.

Arriving on St. George, Maggie continued on 300, which turned into a main drag of sorts, running parallel to the beach and attended to on either side by streams of vacation rentals in various pastels. St. George Island was about 28-miles long and around half a mile wide in most places. The southern eight miles of the island made up the State Park.

After just a couple of miles, she passed through Vacationland and into the stretch of road leading to the 2,000-acre State Park. After half a mile, she came to the pull-off, a spot of asphalt with five or six parking spaces, all of them occupied.

Today, the spots weren't filled with trucks belonging to men doing a little shore fishing. There was Wyatt's cruiser, another car from the Sheriff's department, the Medical Examiner's van, and an apparently unnecessary EMT truck.

Finally, there was a blue Saab that Maggie knew belonged to Gregory Boudreaux, who was reportedly losing his mind on the beach.

Wyatt was leaning against his cruiser when Maggie pulled in. He headed over to Maggie's ten-year old Cherokee as she parked and got out. He was easily six-foot four and, though he was closer to fifty than he was forty, walked toward Maggie's Jeep with the lanky, relaxed gait of a man half his age.

Wyatt had come to Apalachicola from Cocoa Beach a little over six years ago, following his wife's death from breast cancer. Between his widower status, the tinge of gray in his light brown hair and mustache, and his bright blue eyes, he'd quickly become the unconcerned darling of the women of Franklin County. His combination of goofy, self-deprecating humor and movie star looks made him equally popular with men and women.

Maggie knew that, his laid-back approach notwithstanding, Wyatt was smart as a whip and actually took his job pretty seriously, despite the fact that Apalachicola's crime rate made Cocoa Beach look like Detroit.

She grabbed Wyatt's coffee and handed it to him as the wind whipped her long, dark brown hair around her head.

"So, what's the story?" she asked as she yanked her hair into a ponytail.

Wyatt took an appreciative swallow of his coffee before answering.

"Vacationite by the name of Richard Drummond found the body at 8:15 while he was walking his dog. A Golden Retriever mix of some kind. Might be a little Lab in there."

Maggie grabbed her coffee out of the console, handed it to Wyatt and slammed her door before heading to the back of the Jeep.

"When did Larry get here?" she asked, referring to the medical examiner.

She opened the gate and pulled out her crime scene kit.

"About ten minutes ago," Wyatt answered. "He's talking to the deceased now."

"Who got here first?" she asked him, squinting over at the other cruiser.

"Dwight got the call from dispatch, got here at 8:25," Wyatt said. "He called me on the way and I got here a little after 8:30."

He took another swallow of his coffee and held hers out to her.

"No one else has happened on the scene and Dwight's got it taped off. I took lots of pretty pictures for you."

Maggie reclaimed her coffee and took a long swallow before they started walking the twenty or so yards along the path through the sea oats. Wyatt was more than a foot taller than Maggie and she took two steps to his one.

"Are we sure it's suicide?"

"'course not," Wyatt answered. "That's why you're here."

"Couldn't you get Terry to handle it?"

"He's over in Eastpoint working that robbery," Wyatt said. "That's what happens when you're fifty percent of the Criminal Investigation Division, Maggie. You want guaranteed days off, move to Tallahassee."

They reached the beach and Maggie saw the scene about ten feet further east. Larry Wainwright, a hundred years old if he was a day, was perched gingerly in the sand and leaning over the body. Sgt. Dwight Shultz, also known as Dudley Do-right, was keeping the seagulls out of the way by tossing them potato chips a few yards down the beach. The two EMTs stood nearby, with nothing really to do but wait to be dismissed.

Maggie and Wyatt stepped over the yellow crime scene tape and stopped near Gregory Boudreaux's splayed and loafered feet.

"Morning, Maggie," Larry said over his shoulder.

"Morning, Larry," she answered. "So what do we know so far?"

"Well, rigor's set in the face. It is now 9:20," Larry answered, checking his watch. "Between that and body temperature, I'd say time of death was between 6:00a.m.and 6:30."

Maggie finished pulling on her Latex gloves and crouched on the other side of the body with a few baggies in her hand.

A .38 revolver lay next to Gregory Boudreaux's right hand, his thumb still stuck in the trigger guard. She glanced over at Larry.

"Wounds seem consistent with a .38?"

"They do," Larry answered, and gently placed a gloved finger on the chin to turn the face toward him. "As you can see, we have quite the exit wound, which we'd expect from something of that caliber."

"So it appears to be self-inflicted then?"

"I'd say so at this point. I don't see anything at this juncture to argue against it," Larry told her. "As you can see, there's quite a bit of blowback on both hands, as well as residue."

"Kind of unusual, it being so close to the body," Wyatt mentioned noncommittally.

"True, true," said Larry. "The kickback will usually send it flying. But I'd say it stays nearby or even in the decedent's hands about twenty percent of the time."

"You know Gregory Boudreaux, Maggie?" Wyatt asked her.

"Some," she said.

"Can you think of any reason he might want to blow his brains out?"

"I can't really think of any reason why he shouldn't," she said evenly, focusing on Gregory's lifeless right hand. There was a good bit of blood splatter.

"Well, then," Wyatt said. "Can you sugarcoat that more specifically?"

Maggie took a slow breath and removed Boudreaux's thumb from the trigger guard and placed the revolver in an evidence bag. She breathed out only after she'd sealed the bag.

"Not really," she answered finally. "He was just your average Boudreaux, entitled and self-absorbed."

The medical examiner struggled to rise and Wyatt hurried over to give him a hand.

"I've got what I need in the immediate," Larry told them. "I'll take one of those responder boys back to the van to get the body bag. Once we get him up, you'll find most of the rest of the skull fragments are underneath his shoulders. Indicates to me he was seated when the gun was fired. I'll know more in a couple of days."

Larry called for one of the EMTs to come get a body bag, and Maggie watched the old man make his way back toward the parking area before she squinted up at Wyatt.

"Where's the guy that found him?"

"I told him he could go on back to his rental," Wyatt answered. "I took his initial statement. He and the dog left the rental for their walk about 8:00, according to the *Today* show. He didn't hear anything unusual prior to that, no gunshot or anything. You want to talk to him when you're done?"

"How long is he here for?"

"He checks out of the rental on Monday."

"I'll wait. So far, it looks like a straight suicide. I don't see any reason – was there a note?"

"Not so far. Checked his car, but I didn't check his pockets."

Maggie looked down at the body and sighed.

"Getting squeamish in your old age?" Wyatt asked her with a quick smile. She'd only just turned thirty-seven.

Maggie shot him a look, then reached into the right front pocket of Boudreaux's khakis. A set of keys to the Saab and a stick of Dentyne. She bagged them and reached over the body to the other pocket, pulled out the empty bread bag.

Maggie and Wyatt exchanged a look and Maggie looked back toward the path to the parking lot.

"Well, I don't think he left a trail back to his car," Maggie said.

"Dwight said it looked like he'd been feeding the gulls. When he first got here, there were a couple of birds with some splatter on them."

Maggie looked over at Dwight, who had run out of potato chips and was shaking the bag at the remaining few birds, yelling, "Git!"

"Dwight, you think he was feeding the birds?" she called, holding up the bread bag.

"Wouldn't surprise me," he said, flapping his arms. "He liked to come out here a lot."

Maggie frowned at Dwight's back.

"How well did you know him?" she asked. Dwight looked over his shoulder at her.

"I didn't, really," he said. "But back when my brother Rob was still drinking, they used to hang out from time to time. They came out here to fish quite a bit and he told me once that Boudreaux almost always brought something for the seagulls. It bugged Rob, 'cause they'd hang around and try to get at the bait."

"Okay," Maggie said and bagged the bag. Then she looked at the body for a minute before looking just past the head, where a few bits and pieces of skull and hair had been glued to the sand by tacky blood. She looked back at the dead, meticulously manicured hands, and stretched her neck to conceal the shiver that went up her spine.

"Would you mind bagging the hands for me while I get what's on the sand there?" she asked Wyatt.

"Sure."

Wyatt squatted on the other side of the body and set his coffee down behind him while Maggie took some baggies and tape out of her kit. She handed them to him.

"Thanks," she said, not looking up at his face.

She pulled a folding shovel out of her kit, opened it up, grabbed a few more bags and gently scooped up the remains and some sand, placed them in bags without talking further. As she slid the last scoop of sand and brain matter into a bag, a deformed .38 round revealed itself in the depression she'd left.

"Got a bullet," she told Wyatt and picked it up and dropped it into its own bag.

"Did you get to see your kids this morning?" Wyatt asked her.

"Only long enough to walk them to the school bus," she said.

"Sorry about your day off," Wyatt told her. "I know you needed it."

"It's okay," she answered. "I don't think this is going to amount to anything, do you?"

"Doesn't appear that way," he answered.

"Well, then I might still get tomorrow off," she said quietly. "I've got a bunch of squash and peppers to pick for tomorrow."

Two days a week, local gardeners brought produce to Battery Park next to the marina, to be distributed among oyster-fishing families still trying to recover from the latest oil spill. The oysters still hadn't come back to their former numbers and maybe they never would. They'd already been in decline, thanks to the two previous spills and Atlanta's insistence on stealing water from the Apalachicola River to fill its swimming pools.

"I'm assuming Bennett Boudreaux is the next of kin?" Wyatt asked as he handed Maggie her roll of tape.

Maggie looked up at the Sheriff.

"I would say so," she answered. "He was the only child of Boudreaux's only brother. His parents died when he was about twelve, I think. I don't know anything about the mother's family. They're in Mississippi or Texas, something like that."

"Well, notification should be fun," Wyatt answered. "Wanna come?"

"Yeah," Maggie answered distractedly.

"It's a Friday, which one of his businesses should we visit first?"

"He usually works out of the Sea-Fair office," Maggie answered, referring to the plant where Bennett Boudreaux bought, processed, and shipped oysters and Gulf shrimp. "But I hear he doesn't go in all that much anymore."

"Well, then let's try the house," Wyatt told her.

Larry and the EMT came back, carrying a gurney over the deep, powdery sand. They released the legs once they reached the body, and the medical examiner unfolded a black body bag and laid it next to the body.

When the EMTs lifted the body by the shoulders and feet, a small chunk of bloody skull dropped to the sand, joining several other bits of hairy bone in the bloodstained patch of sand that had been beneath Gregory Boudreaux.

It wasn't until the men had the body on the gurney and began zipping the bag that Maggie looked at the face. There were burn marks on one side of the open mouth, and the top teeth that remained looked almost out of place in the bloody mess that surrounded them. Gregory's eyes were closed, a fact for which Maggie was grateful.

Maggie felt a small wave of revulsion creep through her stomach. As the bag zipped shut over his face, she tried to summon some measure of human or at least professional sympathy, but the only thought that came to mind was, *Better late than never.*

⚓ ⚓ ⚓

For a town with one traffic light and a population of fewer than three-thousand people, Apalachicola had a preponderance of historic buildings. Between the old warehouses and quaint shops and cafes downtown along the bay and the residential historic district, there were around nine hundred buildings on the National Historic Register.

The architecture of Apalach was a mixture of Greek Revival and Florida Cracker, brick mansions and squat shotgun houses. Apalachicola often put visitors in mind of a Floridian version of Nantucket. There were quite a few people who had come from up north to spend a weekend and ended up retiring there. There was also a substantial artist community in town.

The result was a town that looked like it was stuck in the past, but which was actually surprisingly progressive in many ways. Fifth-generation oystermen with GEDs had lively discussions with former professors from Yale, and gay activists checked their event schedules with those of the DAR so that Battery Park didn't get overbooked.

Many of the most impressive old houses in town were located just a few blocks from downtown, on the Alphabet Avenues. Bennett Boudreaux's house was among them, on Avenue D.

Among other things, Bennett owned the largest seafood distribution company in Franklin County, shipping Apalach oysters as far west as Colorado and as far north as New York. He also owned trucking companies in both Apalach and Louisiana, several vacation rental houses on St. George, and a few local politicians.

Boudreaux's father had moved here from south Louisiana in the 1960s, gradually turning one oyster boat into a fleet and opening his own seafood business. Bennett had left Apalach to get a degree in finance at Ole Miss, then spent some years in Louisiana, building his businesses from the ground up. He'd come back to Apalach to take over his father's shipping business almost thirty years ago, when his daddy died of a massive coronary. Some people, when they weren't anywhere near Boudreaux, whispered that he'd probably scared the old man to death.

Boudreaux had never been convicted of anything in court, or even arrested for anything. However, he'd been convicted of many things in the minds of most of the law enforcement officers and many of the citizens of Franklin County. He was suspected of running drugs, interfering with unions, bribing judges, funding politicians, and even contracting the odd murder or missing person.

Boudreaux sat on numerous boards, sponsored many events, and even helped judge the oyster-eating contest at the annual Florida Seafood Festival, but more than a few people were more than a little scared of Bennett Boudreaux.

Maggie pulled her Cherokee into the oyster shell driveway in front of Boudreaux's two-story, white house, a wide, wooden home in the Low-Country Plantation style, which sat on a deep lot of almost an acre.

Maggie saw Wyatt pull his cruiser in behind her and she turned off her Jeep and climbed out. As Wyatt made his way over to her, Maggie looked at the front porch that extended all the way around the large but surprisingly unpretentious house. Pots of begonias in every color hung from the porch rafters and larger pots of hibiscus sat on either side of the steps. An array of white wrought iron chairs and tables filled the porch from one end to the other.

Wyatt met Maggie at her car.

"Nice place, huh?" He took off his sunglasses to look up at the house.

Maggie shrugged without commitment and they headed over to the flagstone path, oyster shells crunching beneath their feet. Once they got to the front door, they exchanged a look and Wyatt stepped forward. The white wrought iron screen door squeaked as he opened it to knock on the solid cypress front door. He eased it shut and waited.

A moment later, a light-skinned black woman opened the door and peered at them without much interest. She was in her mid-fifties or so, angular and tall in a flowered housedress and straw slippers. She wore a white half-apron over her dress and was drying her hands on a towel made of French ticking.

Maggie knew Amelia only by sight and only by first name. Boudreaux had brought her and her mother back from Louisiana with him, but no one ever saw the mother anymore and Amelia kept to herself.

"Yes?" Amelia asked them, her voice deep and sandy.

"Is Mr. Boudreaux available, please?" Wyatt asked. "We need to speak with him."

Amelia looked from Wyatt to Maggie, then cut her eyes toward the back of the house.

"Mr. Bennett out back with his mangoes," she told them. "You can walk around."

Wyatt nodded something like thanks, and he and Maggie walked back down the steps, the door closing quietly behind them.

They walked to the side of the house, where they picked up an oyster-shell path through excessively healthy bougainvillea and hibiscus bushes and ended up in a back yard that took up most of the deep, narrow lot.

Beyond a paved patio area just in back of the house, the rest of the lot was devoted to a dense planting of trees. There were coconut palms, bananas, Key Limes, oranges, avocados, and grapefruit, but the entire back of the lot was set aside for at least a dozen large mango trees. Mangoes weren't the easiest thing to grow this far north unless you had the money for heaters and tarps and other means of intervention. Boudreaux did.

In a sunny spot in front of the mango orchard were several rows of mangoes in various sizes and in various pots. This was where they found Bennett Boudreaux

Wearing tan cotton trousers and an untucked white shirt, he was picking yellowed leaves from a young potted tree. He wore dark sunglasses and a straw Panama hat with a yellow band. Wyatt and Maggie crossed the grass and stopped a few feet away.

"Mr. Boudreaux?" Wyatt asked.

Boudreaux looked over his shoulder. He was small in stature, maybe five foot seven, but a youthful and handsome man, even in his early sixties. He removed his sunglasses as he turned to face them, revealing brilliant blue eyes underneath his curious frown.

"Good morning, Sheriff," he said, his voice much deeper than his size led people to expect. Everything about him, from his demeanor to his bearing, made him seem like a much bigger man to those around him, especially those who were not in his good graces. He was unfailingly polite and not given to bluster, but there was a blue collar hardness to him, despite his wealth and education, that intimidated many.

Boudreaux's eyes fixed on Maggie's for just a moment.

"Maggie," he said with a quick nod. Maggie nodded back. "I doubt you've stopped in to say 'hello,'" he said. "Please tell me those boys haven't been messing around in the marina again."

A few weeks earlier, some teenaged boys with a surplus of courage and a deficit of sense had climbed the chain-link at Boudreaux's boat yard and had a little party on one of his shrimp boats. The parents had been more than happy to make restitution, probably relieved that Boudreaux hadn't stopped by personally to collect it.

"No, Mr. Boudreaux, I'm afraid we have some bad news," Wyatt said quietly.

Boudreaux looked Wyatt straight in the eye.

"What is it?"

"Your nephew Gregory's body was found on the beach over on St. George," Wyatt said. "Right now, it appears he shot himself. He's dead."

Maggie watched as Boudreaux's left eye narrowed a bit and he lifted his cleft chin, but there was no other physical evidence of emotion. None was expected; it wasn't his way.

"When did this happen?" Boudreaux asked after a moment.

"Early this morning," Wyatt answered. "About six, six-thirty."

Boudreaux tossed the leaves he was holding into a bucket, then took off his hat, crossed himself, and wiped a forearm across his brow. He looked at his hat for a minute. Wyatt and Maggie waited for him. When he looked up, Boudreaux's eyes were dry and sharp.

"And you think he killed himself," he stated.

"It looks that way, yes." Wyatt took off his sunglasses and wiped at the bridge of his nose. "Did he live here? Did you see him this morning?"

"No, he has a cottage over on Eleventh Street. 746 Eleventh Street," Boudreaux answered. "I think the last time I saw him... yes, it was Tuesday. He came by the warehouse."

"You know if he owned a .38 revolver?" Wyatt asked.

"I couldn't say for certain, but we all have firearms," Boudreaux answered. "I know he had a rifle; we hunt at least once or twice every fall."

"Do you know why your nephew might have wanted to kill himself, Mr. Boudreaux?" Wyatt asked.

Boudreaux took a minute as he squinted up into the mango trees. A drop of sweat coursed from his perfectly barbered hair onto his brow. He touched it away with one finger before looking back at Wyatt.

"I'll be direct with you, Sheriff Hamilton. Gregory didn't make much of an attempt at living."

"How do you mean?" Wyatt asked.

"I mean he was a failure at the few things he was motivated enough to try," Boudreaux answered. "Dropped out of Florida State, got dumped by the two women he proposed to, and probably would have been fired from his job if I didn't own the company."

"So you're not surprised to hear he might have killed himself?" Maggie asked.

Boudreaux turned his gaze to Maggie.

"I am surprised, but I'm not shocked," Boudreaux answered. "I don't care to speak ill of the dead, especially my own family, but Gregory's never been a happy person and most of his unhappiness was his own doing. He was forty years old, and had nothing that wasn't paid for by someone else."

Boudreaux looked from Maggie to Wyatt, then looked down at the ground.

"Even so," he said, "I probably could have done better with him."

"Did you get along alright?" Wyatt asked.

"I'm not that easy to get along with," Boudreaux answered simply.

He ran a hand through his still-thick, brown hair and put his hat back on, cleared his throat.

"Do you know when my nephew's body will be released to the family?"

"I can call and let you know," Maggie answered. "It shouldn't be more than a couple of days if everything's as straightforward as it seems."

Boudreaux looked at Maggie with a touch of gratitude in his eyes.

"Thank you, I'd appreciate that," he said. "Do you need me for anything else at the moment? I'd like to call Father Manero and see about a Mass."

"Do you mind if we take a look at his home, see if he left a note?" Wyatt asked.

"No. I have a spare key in my desk," Boudreaux answered.

"That's alright, we've got his," Wyatt said. "We'll put them back with his effects when we're through."

Boudreaux nodded his thanks, then looked at the ground again. Wyatt was about to say something when Boudreaux looked up and spoke.

"It does surprise me that he shot himself," he said. "Not that he ended his own life, but that he didn't use pills or something."

"Why do you say that?" Wyatt asked.

"Suicide is a cowardly act, but putting a gun in your mouth takes some courage," Boudreaux said.

He looked over at Maggie.

"Gregory didn't have a lot of that."

CHAPTER

TWO

**M**aggie followed Wyatt to Gregory Boudreaux's shotgun cottage, just a few blocks from Bennett Boudreaux's home.

Maggie sat in the Jeep for a moment after she'd turned into the gravel driveway. She took deep breaths of the Jeep's air conditioning and told herself it was the midday heat she was avoiding. Though it was still early June, summer had shown up in a particularly humid mood, and promised to live up to the weather station's prediction of an active hurricane season.

Wyatt stood next to his cruiser, peering at her windshield, so she finally shut off the Jeep and climbed out.

The cottage was respectable without looking particularly important to the owner. The grass was cut and the light blue paint was fairly fresh. The coral hibiscus by the porch steps did what it could to look decorative, but the place still had an air of vacancy to it.

"Think Uncle Bennett owns this place?" Wyatt asked, playing with Gregory Boudreaux's keys.

Maggie shrugged a little and shook her head as she stopped beside him.

"You're unusually quiet today," Wyatt said.

"I've been up since Wednesday morning, remember?" she said. "Is that all?"

"Well, I forgot to pay the electric bill, I miss my kids and I'm spending my day off with dead people. And you," she answered, as they walked toward the front door.

"So there are some positives," he said, and she heard the grin in his voice.

"Sure," she said.

Ordinarily, that would be true. She genuinely liked Wyatt and lately there had seemed to be some undercurrent of mostly playful flirtation between them that she'd found herself enjoying. Today, flirtation and innuendo were the last things on her mind.

Wyatt unlocked the door and they walked into a combination living and dining room, with hardwood floors underfoot and a fireplace on one wall. To the left was a small, outdated kitchen that would have been charming in some other home, and a short hallway led to the back of the house. Brown leather furniture looked expensive but out of place in the living room, and a laptop and piles of papers on the dining room table made it less than welcoming.

"He appears to be single," Wyatt cracked.

Maggie chose not to answer. Instead, she quickly made her way over to the dining room table, mainly in the hope that this would make the bedrooms Wyatt's problem by default.

She pulled a blue pair of Latex gloves from her jeans pocket and slid them on, then poked at a pile of both opened and unopened mail. There were quite a few credit card statements, most of them still sealed. A few pieces of junk mail. Next to the open laptop sat a legal pad with the top few pages folded under.

Maggie heard Wyatt move from the kitchen to the back of the house as she looked at the open page of the legal pad. There were notes about several flight numbers and departure times, but no destinations. The dates were all for tomorrow.

Maggie flipped the pad to the first few pages, but they were filled with doodles, mainly arrows and stars. Apparently, Gregory had been doing some thinking. She wondered if it had hurt. There was no suicide note, although several pages had been ripped off of the pad.

She pressed the power button on the laptop and looked around the room while she waited for it to boot. There was a stuffed marlin over the fireplace, but other than a few rows of liquor bottles on a sideboard, the only other attempt at décor was a picture of Gregory on a fishing boat, flanked by Bennett Boudreaux's two sons.

Patrick Boudreaux was the Assistant State's Attorney and his younger brother Craig made his living in criminal defense. The joke was that Boudreaux had covered all his bases when he sent his boys off to law school.

The Windows screen appeared on the laptop with a jingle, showed the user as Gregory, and politely requested the password. Maggie hit "Enter" just in case, but Windows insisted. She turned the power back off as Wyatt came back from the back of the house.

"Find a note?" he asked her.

"No, but I can't get into the laptop," she answered.

"We'll take it back to the department and see what Jake can do with it," Wyatt said, referring to the department's computer guy.

Maggie pulled the power cord out of the wall and wound it into a loop.

"Well, the only dirty dishes in the sink are coffee cups, there's nothing in the fridge but condiments and there are two empty bottles of Wild Turkey in the trash can," Wyatt said.

He moved over to the dining table and poked at one of the piles of mail.

"Despite the optimism demonstrated in the three-thousand condoms I found in the nightstand, it would appear that our boy didn't entertain anyone other than himself. At least, not here."

Maggie swallowed a bolus of nausea as she closed the laptop and set the cord on top, then walked past Wyatt and down the short hallway to the back. She ignored the bedroom on the right and stepped into the bathroom at the end of the hall.

The bathroom was small and done in light blue tile, probably from the 1950s. A matching pedestal sink sat by the door. Maggie gingerly toed aside a discarded towel and stepped over to open the medicine cabinet.

Aside from a razor, over-the-counter allergy meds, and a tube of toothpaste, there was a half-full bottle of paroxetine hydrochloride prescribed a year ago by a doctor in Tallahassee. Maggie thought it interesting that he'd gone an hour and a half away to get his antidepressant.

She also wondered if the fact that this particular med often made it hard to orgasm was the reason why it was still half-full. Then she felt another push of nausea and wondered what Wyatt would think if she threw up in the sink.

She took the prescription bottle back with her to the living room. Wyatt was looking at the legal pad.

"Looks like our guy was thinking about going somewhere tomorrow," he said as she came in. "Kind of odd. If it was suicide, you think he decided wherever he was going wasn't gonna be far enough?"

Maggie pulled a baggie from her back pocket and held the bottle up before dropping it in.

"What's that?" Wyatt asked her.

"Generic Paxil," she answered. "A year old, from some doctor in Tallahassee. Doesn't look like he took much of it."

"Long way to go for some antidepressants," Wyatt said.

Maggie nodded.

"I'll call the doctor, see if he can tell us about that," she said.

"We can talk to Boudreaux," he said.

"That, too."

Wyatt picked up the laptop.

"We done, you think?" he asked.

"Yeah, for now at least." She wanted outside. "Grab the legal pad, too."

Maggie headed for the door and Wyatt followed. While he locked up, she waited on the front path, grateful now for the heat and the sun.

"It's almost one," Wyatt said as they walked toward the driveway. "I can take this stuff back to Eastpoint if you want to grab a quick nap before your kids get home from school."

She shook her head. "If I go to sleep now, I won't be able to sleep tonight."

"How about if I buy you lunch to make up for calling you in?" He set the laptop and legal pad on his roof and opened his door.

Maggie was pretty sure she'd rather lick a scorpion than put a bite of food in her mouth.

"Sure," she answered.

"AJ's?"

"Okay," she told him as she got in her Jeep.

⚓    ⚓    ⚓

AJ's Neighborhood Grill & Bar was on Fulton, also known as Martin Luther King. It was as nondescript a place as it could be and looked more like an old corner market than a restaurant. It was a local favorite though, much beloved for its soul food, particularly its fried chicken.

Most of the lunch crowd had come and gone, so many of the booths and oak tables in the large, plain space were empty. Maggie and Wyatt both ordered sweet tea and opted to skip the buffet. Wyatt ordered a Pimp Tight basket, a fried chicken breast and wing with a side of fries and green beans. Maggie asked for a small bowl of AJ's famous mac and cheese without actually wanting it.

They made small talk while they waited for their food, first about the weather and then about the softball team Maggie coached and on which her sixteen-year old daughter Skylar played.

"How's David doing these days?" Wyatt asked.

Maggie looked out the window at the gravel parking lot.

"I haven't talked to him in a few weeks," she said.

"Has he talked to the kids?"

"No," she said.

Wyatt nodded, then leaned back in his seat as the young black waitress brought their food.

Maggie had divorced David four years earlier. They'd gone steady since fifth grade and gotten married the weekend after Maggie had graduated from the University of Florida. They'd been married for almost ten years when the BP oil spill had changed their lives.

Against Maggie's better judgment, David had just taken out a large loan for a new shrimp boat. It was repossessed three months after the spill. After several months of no work and no income but hers, David had announced that he had a new job with a trucking company based in Panama City. In actuality, his new job had been running pot between the growers out in Tate's Hell Forest and the buyers in Panama City. David had also started drinking.

David had done six months for simple possession last year. She had pretended to be just as surprised as Wyatt, her friends and her neighbors. The kids, her parents, and her younger brother Mason had known the reason for the divorce. Like her, they mourned the David they'd always known.

"So, I'll go back to the office and have Jake look at the laptop, call this doctor in Tallahassee, see what he says," Wyatt told her. "You go home and I'll let you know if anything interesting turns up."

"Okay," she said, poking her spoon around in her macaroni.

"Are you eating that or just checking it for bones?"

Maggie pushed the dish in his direction.

"I'm too tired to be hungry," she said.

Wyatt took a bite of her mac and cheese, his impressive eyebrows coming together as he frowned at her.

"Hard thing, working and raising kids alone," he said.

Maggie shrugged with one shoulder and looked back out the window at nothing.

"But you're a good woman and halfway decent-looking," he said. "Maybe one day you'll get married again."

Maggie looked at him, but he was newly focused on his green beans. Looking at Wyatt usually made her smile. Sometimes, lately, it sent a warmth through her stomach, curling like smoke from the end of a cigarette. Today, it just made her sad.

"I don't know," she said. "Maybe I'm supposed to be alone."

"I'd hold off betting on that," he said to his beans.

# CHAPTER
# THREE

**M**aggie lived about five miles northwest of downtown Apalach, on the last gravel road that turned off Bluff Road before Bluff Road itself dead-ended in gravel. It was isolated and silent, save for the crickets, cicadas, and frogs.

The two acres on which Maggie's house sat was shaped like a slice of pie, with the narrow tip ending in a dock right on the Apalachicola River. Across the river and on either side of Maggie were nothing but woods of slash pine, live oak and Tupelo.

Maggie parked the Jeep, got out, and stretched her back as Coco, her five-year old Catahoula Parish Leopard Hound, came bounding out from the back of the house. Her one rooster, Stoopid, was running close behind.

Stoopid veered off and headed toward the chicken coop while Coco did her full body wag and licked Maggie's outstretched hands.

"Hey, baby," Maggie said. "How's my girl?"

She knelt down and buried her nose in Coco's neck, breathing deeply of the soothing scents of dirt and brine and fur, then she stood and walked over to the raised beds that ran along one side of the chicken coop.

She'd spent the last two weeks on a murder case that had end-ed with a confession from the ex-husband, a nearly toothless old man with nicotine stained fingers and an inability to adjust to being alone. The garden showed her neglect. Sky and Kyle had tried to keep up, but Sky had final exams to study for. Now that it was the last day of school, maybe Maggie and the kids could get caught up, with the garden and with each other.

She pulled a few wizened pickling cucumbers from their vines and walked over to the small chicken yard, a shady area dominat-ed by a little stilt chicken coop with a green tin roof, a replica of the family house that David and the kids had built six years ago, when everything was the way it was.

The hens, a conglomeration of White Silkies, Buff Orpingtons and Rhode Island Reds, all gathered at the fence while Maggie broke up the cukes and tossed them in. Stoopid, so named for his inability to tell time, flew up to the fence and then hopped in and joined his women.

"Come on, Coco," Maggie said and she and her dog headed for the house.

Maggie's grandfather on her daddy's side had built the cy-press house on stilts in the 1950s. Her parents had chosen to live in town, close to the marina, when they'd married and the house had eventually been given to Maggie and David when they'd wed. Its slightly ramshackle appearance belied the fact that it had withstood many a storm in its lifetime and was as solid as the day it was built.

Maggie walked up the flight of wooden stairs to the porch, Co-co's toenails and dog tags tapping behind her. The porch wrapped around the house and was screened in in back, off of the kitchen. It was Maggie's favorite part of the house and she often sat back there in the evening, watching the sun set over her river.

A small flatboat and her grandfather's old oyster skiff were tied at the dock, and she and the kids often took one of them out to the river to fish. They'd catch striped or sunshine bass, bream or trout, then dress and grill them on the deck. Like Maggie, Sky and Kyle had never eaten a fish that had been dead for more than a few hours.

Maggie pulled the screen door open and unlocked the front door, which opened directly into their small dining area. The house got a lot of natural light and was almost always cooled by a breeze from the river. She and David had added several windows when they'd moved in; both of them preferred replacing storm-shattered windows to living without light and air.

Maggie dumped her purse and keys on the table and walked down the short hallway between the main room and the kitchen. The two kids' rooms were on the right, her room on the left, and a small bath at the end of the hall.

Maggie took off her holster and placed it in her nightstand, kicked off her shoes and walked down to the bathroom.

She splashed a few handfuls of cool water onto her face. On the third handful, she had a flash of Gregory Boudreaux's broken and bloody mouth and she jerked upright and stared at herself in the mirror. She looked like hell. There were dark shadows under her wide-set eyes and the little crevices on either side of her lips seemed deeper. She pulled her ponytail up into a messy bun to get the damp hairs off of her and closed her eyes as a faint breeze from the bathroom window brushed her neck.

*Tell me you love me!*

The words, little more than an angry whisper, came from just behind her right ear. Her head jerked toward her right shoulder reflexively and her eyes shot open. That didn't happen much anymore, but exhaustion and the events of the day had taken their toll. She shut off the water and decided not to look in the mirror anymore.

An hour later, Maggie had picked a backache's worth of squash, zucchini, and tomatoes, and was waiting at the end of their road for the school bus. Coco had come along, as was her habit, and was saving Maggie's life repeatedly by swallowing all of the bees that hung out at the mailbox.

Maggie sipped her sweet tea and wiped the sweat from the back of her neck, dreaming of a shower and what passed for autumn in northern Florida.

The school bus wheezed and banged to a stop just before Maggie slipped into heat stroke, and she smiled as first Kyle jumped out and then Skylar followed less exuberantly.

Kyle looked like his father, with a slight build for his ten years, eyelashes long enough to make noise, and shiny, black hair. Skylar favored her mother more, with hair just a shade lighter and the same green eyes and strong chin. At sixteen, she knew everything and knew it before Maggie did, but she was also witty and strong and fiercely protective of her brother.

Maggie wrapped her arms around Kyle, glad that he was still willing to hug and be hugged in view of his friends. She buried her face in his hair, took a deep whiff of her child and forgot about her day.

Sky would never deign to be hugged in public, but she did give Maggie a smile and some sort of hand signal that Maggie took to be positive in nature. Maggie waved at the bus driver as the bus made a U-turn and headed back the way it had come, then she and the kids headed for the house.

"I feel like I haven't seen you guys in weeks," Maggie said.

"You haven't." Sky lifted her ponytail off of her neck. "Can we go somewhere for dinner, you know, to celebrate that school's out?"

"Oh, baby, I'm so tired," Maggie answered. "I ended up working today."

"I thought you were off," Kyle said.

"I was, but something came up."

"Are you still off tomorrow?" Sky asked.

"I am."

Maggie handed her daughter her tea and Sky took a long, grateful drink and passed it to Kyle.

"Can we do something tomorrow then?" Sky asked.

"Well, I've gotta take some stuff to Battery Park in the morning," Maggie said. "But I thought maybe we could go to the pool after."

"Yeah!" Kyle yelled.

"Do you want to go to the park with me in the morning?"

Kyle just shrugged but Sky's eyes rolled all the way back to her neck.

"Is that supposed to be funny?" she asked. "I'm sleeping in. I'll help you pick the vegetables, though, after I get something to drink."

"I got them, but thanks."

"Regan wants me to spend the night tomorrow night," Sky said.

"I guess it's okay," Maggie said.

"Mommy-son date, then," Kyle said, throwing a rock up the road. "Can we get a movie?"

"Sure, buddy." Maggie brushed a lock of damp hair from her son's eyes. "Don't forget we've got a softball game tomorrow night, Sky."

"I know. She wants me to ride home with her after."

Sky was starting to lose interest in softball, but hung in there because she knew how much her mother loved coaching the team. It was also a decent shot at some scholarship money and they needed that.

Kyle was still enthusiastic about baseball, but less of a player than his sister. He played for fun and he played for his Dad, who had been the high school baseball star in a high school that took baseball very seriously. David had been offered scholarships, but chose fishing shrimp and oysters over an education, just as his father and grandfather had done. Now he didn't have that, either.

They got back to the house and Kyle ran up the stairs, less oppressed by the sticky heat than were his mother and sister, who followed at their own pace. Once they got inside, Maggie turned up the ceiling fans and got some more ice for her tea.

Kyle, predictably, tossed his backpack onto the bench by the door and jumped onto the couch to play Minecraft. Sky followed her Mom into the kitchen and got a glass from the cupboard.

Sky held her glass out to Maggie, who dropped some ice into it, then poured her some tea. Then Sky watched Maggie walk over to the sink and look out the window.

"Are you okay, Mom?"

Maggie turned to look at Sky, who was leaning against the fridge, eyeing her over her tea.

"Sure, sweetie," Maggie answered. "I'm just tired."

"You're lying," Sky said simply.

"Shut up. I don't lie to you guys."

"You do if you think it's 'best'," Sky said with a smirk.

Maggie raised an eyebrow at her daughter.

"So why'd you get called in to work?"

"A body on St. George," Maggie said. "Suicide, probably."

"Serious? Who?"

"I don't want to talk about it, Sky. I'm off duty."

"It'll be in the paper anyway," Sky said.

"Then read it. Now move out of my way. I'm gonna see what we have for dinner."

⚓ ⚓ ⚓

Maggie was at Battery Park by 7:30 the next morning and added their vegetables to the folding tables, upended crates, and tailgates full of produce from other locals.

The gardeners of Apalach had been growing and donating extra produce since the last oil spill, and it was just one more thing that Maggie loved about her hometown and the people in it. When the job started getting to her, she reminded herself of people like old Mrs. Jarrett, who was about nine hundred years old and still managed to bring a hundred pounds of tomatoes and cucumbers and beans every week.

Everyone tried to organize the produce a bit to make it easier on the people who came to choose it as though they were shopping at a farmer's market. Everyone piled their tomatoes with everyone else's tomatoes, their beans with everyone else's beans. It not only made shopping easier for the oystering families, it also kept them from having to know exactly whose cucumbers they were putting in their Publix bags.

Maggie spotted her parents talking with some people across the parking lot and started over there to say "hello." About halfway there, she stopped at an unmarked, white refrigerated truck. Two Hispanic men she didn't know were in the back of the truck, handing cases of cantaloupe out to a couple of local men. On the ground in front of the truck were dozens of watermelons.

Maggie watched the local guys carry a case of melon over to a nearby table, then she looked up at one of the men in the truck.

"These are beautiful," she said. "Where are they from?"

One of the men looked at his friend, then looked back at Maggie and shook his head.

"¿De dónde viene esto?' Maggie asked again.

"No sey," the man said, shaking his head again.

"You brought them here, but you don't know. Okay," Maggie said, shrugging.

As she turned to walk away, she almost ran into one of the local men who were helping unload. She knew his face but couldn't remember his name.

"They're from Boudreaux," he said. "But he asked us not to say anything."

"Bennett Boudreaux?"

"Yeah. From his farm over in Live Oak. He said they were going to go to waste."

"Huh," was all Maggie said, then she headed for her parents.

Gray Redmond was everybody's friend. Though a quiet man, he was universally liked. He was fairly tall and had always been what Maggie's Grandma called "a long drink of water," but he'd become even thinner a few years back when he'd had part of his left lung removed.

The recovery and the chemo that followed it had cost him precious weight and ended his oystering career a bit early, but he was one of the very few people his doctor had ever known to be diagnosed with lung cancer at Stage 1. He was expected to live many more years, and he and his family considered the lost weight and early retirement to be a fair trade.

While Maggie got her love of books and the sea from her daddy, she got her looks from her mother. At fifty-seven, Georgia Redmond still turned heads, though Maggie doubted that she ever noticed. She rarely wore anything more than lip balm and she'd been irretrievably in love with Maggie's father since high school. Her pregnancy with Maggie had rushed their wedding, but it would have happened eventually anyway.

Gray looked up as Maggie approached and stuck out an arm.

"Hey, Sunshine," he said.

"Hey, Daddy." Maggie accepted his hug, then leaned over and kissed her mother's cheek. "Hi, Mom."

"Hi, honey. Do you finally have a day off?"

"I do. Just the one." Maggie smiled and nodded at Jim Fairbanks, who worked for the State Park, and his wife, whose name she couldn't remember. They nodded back.

Georgia lowered her voice and leaned towards Maggie.

"Honey, Jim was just saying that they found Gregory Boudreaux's body on the beach out on St. George."

Maggie glanced over at Jim, who didn't bother looking sheepish. It didn't really matter. The paper didn't come out until Monday, but probably most everyone had heard.

"Yeah, that's right," Maggie said.

"That's a shame," her father said, looking down at the ground.

"He was so young," Jim's wife said, shaking her head but still managing to look titillated.

"He was about your age, wasn't he, Maggie?" Georgia asked. "Did you go to school with him?"

Maggie stared at the space beside her mother's head and wished she was somewhere else.

"No, he was a few years older than me," she said. "I didn't know him."

"Well, I wish he'd done it somewheres else," Jim said quietly. "Tourists don't like it when people shoot themselves all over the beach."

Jim got Georgia's raised left eyebrow, a move Maggie had learned at her mother's knee. Her father noticed it, too, and headed her polite indignation off at the pass.

"Georgia, why don't we go find some shade?" he asked her.

"It was good to see y'all." Jim's wife waved, and Maggie and her parents headed in the direction of Gray's old light-blue pickup.

"He's such a twit," Georgia said under her breath.

"Ah, he's decent enough," Gray said.

"He's just scared," Maggie said. "We need the business."

"The oysters will bounce back," her mother said. "They always do."

Neither Maggie nor her father replied. They both knew that a little less fresh water and a little more oil could finish the Apalach oysters for good.

"What are you guys doing today?" Maggie asked instead.

"We're gonna try to get some work done on the deck, if it doesn't rain too hard later," Georgia said.

"Should be finished by Tuesday," Gray added.

"Why don't we grill out Wednesday night?" Georgia said. "We can have a tournament."

Maggie's family regarded Scrabble with the gravity that some people reserved for fine art or politics. Every game was a tournament.

"That sounds good, Mom," Maggie said. "I'll let you know for sure if I can make it."

"Do you good," Gray said.

"I'm sure it would." Maggie reached over and hugged her father. "I've got to get home. I'll see you later, Daddy."

"See you later, Sunshine."

Maggie hugged her mother and bid her goodbye, then headed for her Jeep.

She looked up at the sky as she opened her door. Dark clouds were rolling in from the west and there was faint hint of ice or metal in the air. Maggie caught it on her tongue and closed her eyes for just a moment, then got in the car.

# CHAPTER
# FOUR

**M**aggie pulled into Piggly-Wiggly, the town's only grocery store and only slightly larger than a really good 7-11. Once a month, she made the drive to Publix an hour away, but the Pig was okay for the occasional quick stop. It was also across the street from the Apalachicola Police Department, a tiny, light-blue building that looked more like a day care center than a center of law and justice.

She climbed out of the Jeep and headed toward the entrance, planning to grab some root beer and vanilla ice cream for her movie night with Kyle. Halfway to the door, she spotted Richard Alessi coming out.

Alessi was a fairly small-time meth dealer who was two strikes out. The last time he'd gone to prison, Maggie had been the one to put him there. It had pretty much soured any chance they'd develop a friendship, but Maggie hadn't cried long.

There was the average lunatic, and then there was the lunatic who self-medicated with coke or meth. Alessi was the latter. When he was fifteen, he'd hung the neighbor lady's cat just for fun. Maggie was of the opinion that someone should have shot him then. Now thirty-five, he was twenty years crazier and had the dangerous notion that most of his crimes would go unknown and unpunished.

Alessi was wearing his usual uniform of tattered jeans and a biker vest, though he'd never owned a motorcycle. His longish, dark brown hair looked eight days unwashed and he had several days' growth of beard. He stopped just outside the doors and bent his head to light the cigarette already dangling from his mouth.

As Maggie continued walking in Alessi's direction, a young girl followed Alessi out the door. She was carrying an infant that couldn't have been more than a month old, and had a little post-natal pooch on her otherwise skinny frame. She held the hand of a little girl of about three, who held the hand of a little boy about four.

The procession stopped behind Alessi and since they were all blocking the door somewhat, Maggie stopped in front of him. He got his cigarette lit and looked up at her.

"Oh, look. It's Lieutenant Dan," he said in a fairly decent Forrest Gump.

"Hello, Richard," she said.

"You here for me? 'Cause I ain't doin' anything."

"No, I'm here for some ice cream. You can wait."

"Naw, you can wait, hun." He blew a lungful of smoke in her direction. She refused to wave it away. "You can wait a good while, 'cause I've been keeping my nose clean."

Maggie looked over at the girl. She looked either embarrassed or afraid. She couldn't be more than eighteen or so, but the kids' clothes and faces were clean and they looked well-fed. Maggie thought about Sky being attached to someone like Alessi, even having his babies, and wondered why no one had snatched this child out of harm's way.

"Your nose has never been clean, Richard," Maggie said.

"Maybe I'm just smart, then," he said back, grinning around his cigarette.

"I think you've just been lucky," Maggie said, smiling kindly. "I've eaten sandwiches smarter than you."

He took a couple of lazy steps toward her, no doubt finding himself menacing. Maggie was intelligent enough to know he was dangerous, but even he wasn't stupid enough to try anything in front of the police department. She stood her ground. If for no other reason, then just in case the girl needed to see it could be done.

Alessi bent just enough to get eye to eye with Maggie. He smelled of Miller, smoke, and meanness.

"I think you're the one that's been lucky, *Miss* Redmond."

"Maybe. But somebody's going to do you in one day and the only one who'll miss that party is you."

He lifted her a slow bird and she stepped around him casually. She looked at the girl, whose eyes were frightened beneath a slash of damp, dishwater bangs.

"What's your name?" Maggie asked her.

"Grace," the girl said softly.

"Don't talk to her. She ain't none of your business," Alessi said behind Maggie.

"You can do better, Grace," Maggie said and headed for the door.

"Get in the car!" she heard Alessi say. She turned around and looked.

Alessi tossed a look over his shoulder as he herded his little group across the parking lot. As Maggie turned back to go into the store, she noticed two cops standing out in front of the station. Andy Thorn, a twenty-year veteran, was smoking a cigarette and waving. Josh Burke, a new recruit, had his hand on his holster.

Maggie waved back at Andy, then went into the Pig.

⚓ ⚓ ⚓

The distant rumble of thunder woke Maggie about eleven o'clock.

She was lying on the couch and Kyle was sitting with his legs over hers, his feet on the old trunk they used as a coffee table. Coco's tags jingled as she stood up from where she'd been sleeping beside the couch. Maggie scratched her ear and looked over at Kyle.

His head was back on the pillow, and a soft snore came from his nose. The TV screen was bright blue and she wondered if he'd made it to the end of their second Redbox movie.

She sat up and slid her legs out from under Kyle's, then brushed a lock of silky black hair out of his eyes.

"Kyle," she said softly.

There was a momentary pause in his snoring and his thick dark lashes quivered, but he didn't wake up. She took the opportunity to run her fingers through his hair, just as she had his whole life, just as she had his father's. He looked so much like David that sometimes her breath caught when he smiled at her. Sometimes her heart broke again, too.

"C'mon, buddy." Maggie shook his shoulder and he stirred, opened his eyes halfway. "Let's get you to bed."

"Unkay," he said, then closed his eyes.

Maggie laid him down on the couch, grabbed a throw from the chair behind her and unfolded it over his legs. Then she turned off the TV, picked up their root beer float glasses, and started for the kitchen.

Coco took a few steps to follow, but Maggie stopped.

"No, you stay with Buddy tonight, okay?"

Coco whined, but jumped up on the couch and curled up at Kyle's feet.

Maggie walked into the dark kitchen and put the glasses in the sink.

The sky grumbled again as she filled the glasses with hot water. She left them for morning, and after checking that the doors were locked, she headed for bed.

⚓ ⚓ ⚓

*Maggie's face was pressed hard into the dirt and three inches of musty autumn leaves. Sticks and at least one rock cut into her left cheek.*

*The ground, and the weight on her back, made it hard for her to breathe. She was sure that her heart was pounding too hard to let her live, and her chest was on fire. Everything was on fire and yet she was so cold.*

*"Tell me you love me!" he said, his hot breath blowing like a dragon's on her right ear.*

*She kept her lips tightly shut, her nostrils flaring as she tried to get enough air without opening her mouth. She could see her fishing rod a few feet away where she'd dropped it, the one Daddy had given her for getting straight A's last semester. He didn't know where she was, didn't know she needed him, and she closed her eyes as hot tears flooded them again.*

*"Tell me you love me!" he insisted again. She felt another sharp pain and her mouth flew open. She intended to tell him what he wanted to hear, but suddenly her throat felt like someone had scraped it with a nail file. She didn't hear, didn't even realize she was screaming, until the weight came off of her and she heard him yell "Shut up!"*

*He flipped her over roughly and she felt herself getting ready to scream again, against her own will. The sight of him stopped her. His shirt was hanging open, his pants around his thighs, and he was holding a rock the size of a basketball over his head.*

*She was fifteen and nobody knew she was way back in the woods. She was going to die in the dirt and the moldy leaves, and Daddy's heart was going to break.*

*She clamped a hand over her own mouth and willed herself not to scream anymore.*

*Gregory Boudreaux slammed the rock down right next to her head and laughed. Then he leaned down to kiss her neck.*

Maggie sat straight up in bed, her right hand pressed so tightly against her mouth that she could taste blood.

Coco was standing on the bed, crying, her back hairs standing straight up like dried grass.

Between the pounding of her own heart and the pounding of the rain on the tin roof, the room was filled with noise.

Maggie took her hand away from her mouth and brushed at her lip with her tongue, tasting salty blood and tears. She took a few deep breaths, then put her arms around Coco's neck, and buried her face in the dog's fur. Coco sat and whimpered as Maggie waited for her heart to slow down, for the smell of molding, wet leaves to be washed from her nostrils.

Finally, she lifted her face, kissed the side of Coco's head and swung her legs over the edge of the bed. It had been a long time since she'd had the nightmares and the flashbacks, but she knew there would be no more sleep tonight.

She looked over at her .45 on the nightstand, the glow from her alarm clock casting an orange light on the grip. It was 3:22 a.m. She picked up the gun and her cell phone, and walked into the living room with Coco at her heels.

First Maggie checked to make sure that Kyle was still sleeping safely on the couch. He was, one forearm thrown over his face. Then she got a glass of water from the kitchen tap and drank it down, one thread of the cool liquid running down her chin and neck.

Maggie walked back into the living room, lifted Kyle's head and sat down, putting his head in her lap. Coco jumped back onto the couch and sat on Kyle's feet.

Then Maggie put her weapon down on the end table and waited for morning.

CHAPTER
FIVE

t was Monday. Maggie had spent the last two days interviewing Gregory Boudreaux's associates, taking the statement of
the man who'd found his body, and talking to Gregory's psychiatrist in Tallahassee, who was distractedly saddened to
hear of Gregory's death, but not especially surprised. He'd treat-
ed Gregory off and on for several years.

Maggie was hanging up the phone when Wyatt walked into
the office she shared with Lt. Terry Coyle, the only other investigator in the Franklin County Sherriff's Department.

Wyatt was drinking a Mountain Dew and had a bulky manila
envelope in his free hand.

"Whatcha doin'?" he asked.

Maggie rolled her head to loosen up her neck and put her pen
down.

"I just finished checking all those flight numbers," she said.
"It looks like Boudreaux was trying to decide between Costa Rica
and Brazil. Either way, he was looking at flights for last Saturday."

"Huh. Well, looks like he decided to go another way. Larry just sent over the autopsy report and Boudreaux's effects. Official decision for suicide."

"Okay then," Maggie said.

Wyatt sat down in the metal folding chair she and Terry used for company, his long legs stretched out in front of him. He tossed the manila envelope onto her desk.

"Thought maybe you could run this over to Uncle Bennett when you're done."

Maggie looked up at the wall clock, which said it was almost four-thirty. Her shift typically ran from 7 a.m. to 5 p.m., unless something important happened. The deputies and Apalachicola PD handled most of the crimes in the area, which were generally fights and burglaries and violations of parole.

She looked at the envelope.

"I don't suppose you could take it. You live like five blocks from Boudreaux."

"Nope."

"Why not?"

"Because one day you'll probably be the Sheriff, but today you are not," Wyatt said. "And besides, I have a dentist appointment."

"I'll bet you're a lot of fun in the dentist's chair."

"I'm told I am," Wyatt said. "The cute little hygienist is named Heather and she thinks I'm a riot. She also admires my gums."

"Your gums are okay," Maggie told him.

"I work out."

"Alright, so I'll do the paperwork on Boudreaux and then I'll take this stuff over to his uncle. Anything else you need from me?"

Wyatt looked at her for a moment that was just long enough to make her a little nervous, and to remind her that he really was extremely handsome.

"No, that's it for now," he said, then broke into a big, dimpled smile as he stood.

"I have to go brush my teeth. Heather disapproves of Mountain Dew."

"Well, I wouldn't want you to disappoint little Heather," Maggie said.

He stopped in the doorway and looked at her.

"Oh, I think I probably will anyway."

He winked at her, then walked out of her office. Maggie watched where he'd been for a moment, willing the slight tingling in her stomach to postpone itself for another time.

Then she looked down at the envelope on her desk and sighed.

"Mr. Boudreaux?"

"Yes?"

Maggie held the cell phone with her shoulder as she backed out of her parking space.

"This is Maggie Redmond. The medical examiner has released your nephew's personal effects. I thought I would drop them off to you on my way home, if it's convenient."

"Where are you?" Boudreaux asked. He sounded like he was outdoors.

"I'm just leaving my office in Eastpoint."

"Well, I just tied in at Boss Oyster," Boudreaux said. "Can you meet me here?"

Boss Oyster was a raw bar just a few blocks north of Battery Park. It was right on the river, on the channel that ran past Big Towhead Island and out to the bay. It was one of Maggie's favorite places to eat.

"Maggie? Lt. Redmond?"

"Yes sir, that'll be fine. I'll be there in about fifteen minutes."

"I'll see you when you get here then."

Maggie heard him disconnect, but she tapped on the phone with her fingernail a few times before she closed it and pulled out of the parking lot.

⚓ ⚓ ⚓

Boss Oyster was housed in a bright green building that looked like a little cottage, guarded by two fan palms, and dwarfed by the warehouses on either side. The warehouses, one of them belonging to Boss, had a derelict appearance that Maggie thought enhanced the place's appeal.

Maggie pulled into the oyster shell parking lot and grabbed the manila envelope before stepping out of the car.

Thunder rumbled overhead and close by, and the air had acquired a quality that Maggie had never experienced outside Florida. It was at once cool and hot, damp and perceptibly electric. This wasn't going to be the usual 3:15 summer rain.

In front of the warehouse next door, a metal sign swung back and forth on its metal rod, sounding like a child's first attempt at the violin.

Maggie walked in and paused in the doorway for a minute to let her eyes adjust to the dimness. She spotted Bennett Boudreaux on the deck in back as one of the servers approached her.

"Hey, Maggie," she said.

"Hey, Delores, good to see you"

"You, too," Delores answered, waving at a table that was flagging her down. "Mr. Boudreaux said you're meeting with him? He's out on the porch."

"Yeah, I see him," Maggie answered. "Can I have a sweet tea when you get a minute?"

"Sure, hon, I'll be right out."

Maggie nodded or waved at a few people she knew as she crossed the room, then pushed open the screen door to the mostly covered deck. The wind gave a little resistance, but the screen door scraped open just as a blue bolt of lightning struck out on Big Towhead Island.

A young tourist couple squeezed past Maggie as they carried their beers and baskets to safety indoors, leaving just Maggie and Boudreaux on the deck. Wearing loose cargo pants and a blue chambray shirt that matched his eyes, he stood up as Maggie walked to his table.

"Maggie," he said.

"Mr. Boudreaux," she answered.

He waited for her to be seated, then sat back down in his chair. A bottle of beer from one of the local micro-breweries sat in front of him, sweating drops of condensation into a small ring on the wooden table.

Maggie put the envelope down on the chair beside her and pulled her own chair in.

"If you like, we can move inside," Boudreaux said.

"Not on my account, please. I like being outside during a storm."

Boudreaux's eyes glinted with a hint of approval.

"So do I. It's invigorating and, at the same time, humbling."

He looked out at the docks, where the boats were getting agitated. One of them was his restored 1947 Chris Craft Express Cruiser, which Maggie would have eloped with given the chance.

"Caught some nice redfish this afternoon, but the swells were getting a little aggressive for the *Parish Princess.*"

The screen door squeaked open and slapped shut, and Delores appeared with Maggie's tea.

"Thanks, Delores," Maggie said.

"Are you sure you wouldn't like a cocktail or a beer or something?" Boudreaux asked her.

"No, thanks. I'm still on duty."

"Oh, yes, sorry."

"Are y'all ready to order?" Delores asked them.

Boudreaux looked at Maggie.

"Oh, nothing for me," Maggie said.

"Please. I wouldn't be able to eat in front of you and I really want some oysters."

Maggie hesitated for a moment, then shrugged. "Okay."

"How do you like 'em?" Boudreaux asked.

"Straight up."

"Good girl," he said with the hint of a smile. "We'll take two dozen raw then, thank you."

"Alrighty, we'll have those out in just a minute," Delores said, and hurried back inside.

"I think whoever invented Oysters Rockefeller should have been hung by the neck until dead," Boudreaux said, taking a swallow of beer. "If you need cheese on an Apalach oyster you don't deserve to eat one."

Maggie didn't really want to smile at the town gangster, so she suppressed it by looking at the envelope and picking it up.

"Here are your nephew's effects," she said, handing the envelope across the table.

"Thank you," Boudreaux said, but while he took the envelope, his eyes never left hers.

He opened the envelope and glanced inside, then closed it again. He looked her in the eye as he tapped the envelope on the edge of the table for a moment.

"Ugly business, this," he finally said.

Maggie nodded. "Yes."

"All of it," he said, still staring.

The addendum made her uncomfortable and she wondered for the first time if he knew what had happened twenty-two years ago. The idea unsettled her, but she didn't look away.

"I'm sorry for your loss," she lied.

He nodded, then looked at the envelope again as though he'd realized he was staring, though Maggie knew it was intentional. She just didn't know why.

Delores arrived then with two round, stainless steel platters of oysters, lemons and crackers. Maggie slowly let out a breath as she set them on the table.

"Can I get you guys anything else?"

"You know what, Delores?" Maggie said. "I think I'll have a vodka and cranberry."

"Sure thing, hon," and Delores was gone.

"Change your mind?" Boudreaux asked.

Maggie held up the wrist on which she wore her Timex.

"I just went off the clock," she lied again.

Boudreaux nodded and placed a napkin on his lap.

For a minute or two, they busied themselves with squeezing lemons and unwrapping packets of saltines.

"Did you and my nephew know each other?" Boudreaux asked, focused on choosing his hot sauce from several bottles on the table. The question sounded like polite conversation, but too much like polite conversation to actually be the thing.

"Not at all," Maggie said to her lap as she spread out her napkin.

Boudreaux tapped exactly one drop of Tabasco onto an oyster, then slurped the oyster out of its shell, his eyes on Maggie all the while. She felt them as she took her first oyster with just the lemon. Then she looked up at him and they watched each other chew.

"Do you agree with the medical examiner that Gregory committed suicide?"

Maggie swallowed before answering.

"I don't really have anything to tell me otherwise," she said. "Do you?"

"Not really," he answered.

"I talked to his psychiatrist over in Tallahassee," Maggie said. "I did find it surprising that Gregory gave him permission to discuss his treatment with you."

"It was a condition of me paying for it for years," Boudreaux said.

"Well, I appreciate you sending him the release."

Boudreaux nodded. "Was he of any help?"

Maggie put down her seafood fork before answering.

"I suppose he was. He said that your nephew had seen him irregularly for about seven years. That he was treating him for depression but had also diagnosed him with Narcissistic Personality Disorder."

Boudreaux picked up his beer and took a leisurely swallow, watching Maggie over the bottle. She watched back.

"What does that tell you?" he asked as he put down his beer.

"That he was a narcissist."

Boudreaux regarded her with something that might be irritation but could just as easily be respect. He was about to say something when Delores arrived with Maggie's drink. They both sat back as though to make room.

"Here you go, hon," Delores said.

"Thank you."

"Thank you, Delores," Boudreaux said politely.

"Y'all sure you don't want to come inside? This storm looks like it's about to break hard."

Boudreaux looked up at Delores.

"It certainly is," he said. "And when it does, it's really gonna be something."

Maggie looked at Boudreaux. "I'm fine where I am."

He smiled and spread his hands. "Then so am I," he said.

"Alright," Delores said, shaking her head. "I'll be back out to check on ya."

Maggie took a healthy swallow of her drink without looking like she needed it, and Boudreaux busied himself popping an oyster onto a saltine. The wind was blowing his quite attractive hair hither and yon, and he ran a hand back through it as he chewed. Behind him on the river, lightning painted blue and white stripes on the water.

Maggie had just slurped another oyster when Boudreaux finally spoke again.

"How's your father doing these days?"

Maggie was surprised by the question and happy for the excuse of chewing her food.

"He's doing well," she said after swallowing.

"I always liked Gray. I was sorry when we had to stop doing business."

"He still goes out to his favorite beds a few days a week," she said. "But he takes them over to the farmer's market in Panama City. He doesn't take enough to wholesale them."

Boudreaux nodded as though in agreement with her father's business sense.

"No oysterman ever really stops," he said. "I still go out, but I fish. It doesn't seem right to take the oysters from someone else."

Maggie watched him fix another oyster on a cracker and put it neatly into his mouth. He noticed her watching as he sat back.

"What?" he asked.

"I was just wondering. You gladly take a public 'thank you' for donating $10,000 to the museum, but you didn't want anyone to know you sent a truckload of melons to Battery Park."

Boudreaux nodded once, then folded his arms on the table.

"When I do something nice publicly, it's because it's the right thing to do for my reputation. When I do it privately, it's because it's the right thing to do."

Maggie felt something very like respect begin to form for the man and she wondered when she'd lost her mind. Aside from the fact that she knew he was guilty of any number of criminal activities, she also knew that there was some kind of spider and fly thing going on at their table, and that she was not the spider.

And yet, the manners and the startling blue eyes and the weird brand of honesty. She had to admit that he was compelling.

"What kind of reputation are you going for?" she asked him, mainly for something to say.

He smiled at her.

"I guess that depends on which business I'm promoting at the time. What kind of reputation are you going for?"

"Integrity, I suppose," she said.

"I admire integrity," he said. "Even when it's inconvenient."

"Am I inconveniencing you in some way?"

"Not thus far."

One side of her mouth turned up in a half-grin and she allowed it. She got one in return.

"Well, you're probably not doing much for my reputation," she said.

"Why's that?"

Maggie glanced over at the nearest window.

"I can only imagine what people think about you and me sitting out here alone," she said.

He put his beer down and leaned onto the table.

"Let me tell you something I've learned," he said. "When you start caring too much about what people think, you give them fractional ownership of your life. I don't believe in fractional ownership."

Just then, the sky opened up and rain exploded onto the deck like musket balls. Their table was under the canopy, but a sheet of cool moisture, fine as organza, brushed up against Maggie's face. She couldn't help but close her eyes in pleasure for just a second. When she opened them, Boudreaux was smiling at her and he looked downright kind.

"So what do you believe in?" she asked him.

"Hard work. God. Family. You?"

Maggie nodded. "The same."

"Nothing is ever black or white, is it?" he asked her. "And nobody's ever all bad or all good."

Maggie swallowed as they looked at each other across the table. He broke the tension with another wink.

"Not often, no." Maggie looked at her watch. "Speaking of family, I need to get going."

Boudreaux stood as she scooted her chair back and got up from the table.

"I'll pay for my check on the way out," she said.

"Don't embarrass me," he said. "I asked you to come."

"Okay. Well, thank you, then," she said.

"Thank you." He watched her pick up her purse. "Oh, Gregory's Mass is Wednesday, if you'd like to come."

Maggie stopped short, her purse halfway up her arm.

"I'm sorry," she managed. "I'm working."

"It's alright. I mainly asked to be polite," he said. "I didn't actually expect to see you."

His eyes had gotten that shrewd, speculative look again, like he was trying to see the other side of her skin.

"Goodbye, Mr. Boudreaux."

"Goodbye, Maggie."

Maggie hurried through the restaurant and waved at Delores as she opened the door. When she looked over her shoulder, Boudreaux was still standing at the table, and still watching her.

She ran to the Jeep, the rain plastering her hair to her head and her clothes to her body within seconds. She yanked open the door and jumped in, closed it quickly behind her.

The rain pounded on the roof at a deafening volume, yet she could hear water dripping from her hair onto the seat. She felt almost as though she'd just gotten back from some alternate universe, and was glad for the tangible reminders that she was still on her own planet.

There was something about Boudreaux that drew her, she had to admit that. But she also had to admit that he'd never said more than five words to her before Saturday, and almost all of those had been "Hello."

A part of her wondered if he knew about Gregory. Another part of her thought that maybe he'd just told her that he did. She couldn't help worrying about why.

She thought back to that day in Boudreaux's backyard and his surprise that Gregory had had the guts to use a gun.

He'd looked at her when he'd said it.

# CHAPTER
## SIX

**M**aggie was waiting at the town's one traffic light when her personal cell phone rang from the passenger seat. She picked it up, saw the call was coming from Wyatt's personal phone, and answered.

"Hey."

"What the hell are you doing sucking down aphrodisiacs with a certain person?" he asked, sounding only mildly aggravated.

"How do you know this already?"

"Because I'm a senior law enforcement officer with almost thirty years on the job," he said. "And because I ran into two different people who were there before I even got to the dentist."

Maggie heard him put his hand over the phone and say, "Excuse me, I'll be in there in just a second."

"How's Heather?"

She heard a door shut.

"She'd like me to get off my phone so she can peer at my gums," he said.

Maggie was pretty sure from the echo that Wyatt had ducked into a bathroom. Or a closet.

"So shut up," she said, smiling.

"What's up with you and Boudreaux?"

"That's where he wanted me to meet him. And I was hungry."

Her light turned green and she turned right onto 98, headed for her parents' house.

"When peace officers are feeling peckish, they're supposed to eat with other good guys, not do a scene from *Goodfellas* at the local raw bar. People are going to start thinking he's grooming you to be his next pet cop."

It was fairly widely believed that her predecessor, Gordon Bellows, had been on Boudreaux's payroll for many years. He was now retired to a nice condo in Key Largo.

"Well, no good guys invited me," she said. "Besides, I needed to drop the stuff off to him. Are you actually mad?"

"No, although I am somewhat put out," Wyatt said. "But I called primarily to deliver a message."

"From who?"

"Some girl named Grace," he said. "She said it was urgent that you call her before six."

It took Maggie a second to place the name.

"Did you talk to her?"

"No, but I told Carla I'd pass it on."

"Okay. Can you text me the number?"

"I don't text. I write or speak."

"Well, could you speak me the number then? I'm driving."

"Hold on. Alright, it's 340-2291. You got it?"

"2291. Got it."

"Okay, well then I'm going to go flex my gums."

"Okeydokey," Maggie said and hung up.

She pulled over to the curb and dialed the number. It was answered halfway through the second ring.

"Hello?"

Grace's voice was small and delicate, and Maggie could barely hear her over the rain thumping her roof.

"Grace? This is Lt. Redmond returning your call."

She heard a sigh at the other end of the line.

"Hey. I was wondering if you could meet me so I could talk to you."

"Do you need help?"

There was a long silence.

"Grace? Do you need help?"

"Well, I was thinking maybe I could help you and that would help me."

"Okay. When do you want to meet?"

"Now. I don't get all that much time away from Ricky and he's gonna expect us back at the house by 6:30."

"Where are you?"

"Battery Park. I'm in my car by the playground. The storm came up on us."

"Do you need me to get you somewhere? To take you somewhere right now?"

"No," Grace answered. "But it's really important."

"What kind of car?"

"It's a blue Monte Carlo."

"Okay, I'm just a few blocks away," Maggie said. "I'll be there in a minute."

"Okay."

Maggie hung up and then speed-dialed the non-emergency number for the Apalachicola PD.

"Apalachicola Police Department, this is Sgt. Frank speaking."

"Hey, Stuart, it's Maggie Redmond."

"Hey Maggie, what's up?"

"I'm meeting someone at the playground in Battery Park. It's probably cool, but could you have one of the guys drive by once or twice anyway?"

"Sure thing. You want him to park just in case?"

"No, it's probably fine, but it's Richard Alessi's girlfriend, so there's a small chance it's hinky. She's in a blue Monte Carlo."

"No problem," Stuart answered. "Doug's over that way. I'll have him keep special eyeballs out for Ricky."

"Thanks, Stuart."

Maggie hung up, made a U-turn and headed for the park. During the five block ride, she called her Mom to let her know she'd be a few minutes late picking up the kids, who had gone fishing with her Dad at Lafayette Pier.

There were a few cars parked near the playground, all of them empty, except for a 1970s Monte Carlo. Through the rain, Maggie could make out Grace in the driver's seat and at least one toddler head in the back seat.

She parked a few cars away, touched the grip of her .45 out of habit, and then got out. The rain was blowing sideways now, and Maggie shielded her face as she walked to the Monte Carlo's passenger side.

She looked in the window, saw the three kids in the backseat in their car seats, no one on the floor. She opened the door and slid into the passenger seat, then slammed the door shut against the rain.

Grace looked pale and small. She had her back to her door and was still holding her cell phone in her hands. She flipped it over and over in her lap. Maggie looked back at the kids. The baby was facing backwards and apparently asleep. The little girl and boy were watching a video on an iPad that the girl held between them. They barely looked up at her.

"Hey, kids," Maggie said anyway.

The little girl blinked at her before going back to her movie. The boy gave her the hint of a smile before putting his head back down on his sister's shoulder.

"Hey, Grace."

"Hey. Thank you for coming, ma'am."

"What's going on?"

Grace looked down at her phone for a minute and seemed to collect herself. When she looked back up at Maggie, her eyes were still wide and afraid but she was sitting up straighter.

"I need to get away from him," she said.

"What do you want me to do?"

"I want you to send him back to jail." She flipped her phone a few more times. "He said if he goes back again, he's going for a long time. Is that true?"

"Yes. How long depends on what he goes up for, but it'll be a while. Three strikes. What do you want me to arrest him for?"

Grace looked back at the kids before answering, her voice lowered.

"He's got something going on Thursday night. I'm not sure what yet, but it's supposed to be something pretty big. Like, more than they usually deal with."

"Okay." Maggie waited.

"He works with Joey Truman and Gary Barone, do you know them?"

"I know Joey."

"Well, they're supposed to come over tomorrow sometime to talk about it. I'll probably know more about what's going on then. I could call you."

"Okay," Maggie said without commitment.

"But, I need to know, you know, would I get in trouble?" Grace looked at the kids again, but they were engrossed in their video. "Can you make it so I don't get in trouble for knowing about all this stuff? 'Cause that makes me like an accessory or something, right?"

"I need to talk to someone in the State's Attorney's office," Maggie said. "But we work with informants all the time. I'm sure we can keep you out of it."

"Can you check to make sure?"

"Yes. But why don't you just leave? Can you take your kids somewhere?"

"Well, but Tammi and Jake aren't mine, they're Ricky's kids. I can't just take 'em."

"Where's their mother?" Maggie asked quietly.

"I don't know," Grace whispered back. "He said she ran off two years ago, but, you know...I think maybe..."

Grace looked into the backseat again to make sure the kids weren't listening. Maggie sighed.

"Where are you from, Grace?"

"Santa Rosa. That's where I met Ricky. He came into the Denny's where I worked."

"Can you go home to your family after?"

Grace smiled, but it wasn't a happy smile.

"My mom died a long time ago and my Dad's worse than Ricky."

Maggie looked at her for a moment.

"How old are you?"

"I just turned nineteen."

"Why are you with someone like him?"

The girl shrugged her bony shoulders.

"I'm not pretty. I'm not even interesting," she said. "I knew he probably wasn't a good person, but it seemed kind of exciting at first."

"Does he hurt you?"

"Sometimes," she said, like it was normal. "The thing is, I can't lose these kids. His, I mean. They need me. If he goes away, nobody else is gonna want 'em. I'll have time to figure something out."

Maggie stared out the windshield for a moment. Through the rain, she could just see a black-and-white cruising slowly down Water Street, across the playground. She looked back at Grace.

"Isn't he going to wonder why you aren't home yet, with the rain?"

"Naw. He knows I'm scared to drive in it. He's probably just glad they're still out of the house. But I gotta get home and get his supper."

"Okay, look. I'll talk to the Assistant State's Attorney and my boss. You call me whenever you know something tomorrow and I'll let you know what they say. But you need to be careful, okay?"

Grace nodded.

"Don't call me if he's anywhere around."

"I won't. He doesn't even know I have this phone. I got it at 7-11. I keep it in the kids' toy box."

Maggie almost smiled. This child might not be well educated, but she was smart. Maggie wanted her to be okay.

"Okay," she said, putting her hand on the door handle. "You need to get home. I'll wait for your call, all right?"

"Okay."

Maggie started to open the door, then glanced at the back seat and back at Grace.

"They're not going to say anything to him about you meeting me, are they?"

"They don't talk to him," Grace said quietly.

Maggie wanted to get to her parents' and hug her kids. She wanted to take these four kids with her.

"Okay, I'll talk to you tomorrow, okay?"

"Yes, ma'am. Thank you."

Maggie got out of the car and ran for her Jeep. The rain had let up somewhat, but she was soaked through and cold, despite the temperature.

She climbed into her vehicle, started the engine, and turned on her heat. While she waited for the warmth to show up, she watched the Monte Carlo pull out and slowly turn right onto 6th Street.

Maggie backed out and waited at the road for a pickup truck to pass by. As she sat there, the patrol car came by from the other direction. Maggie rolled her window down and waved and Doug Petrie, a friend from high school, waved back and went on his way.

Maggie pulled out and headed for family, warmth and normalcy.

⚓ ⚓ ⚓

*Maggie had her right hand clamped so tightly over her mouth that she could feel the outline of every one of her upper teeth on her lip. In her left hand, she squeezed a clump of rocks and twigs.*

*She couldn't seem to breathe fast or deeply enough and the air whistled out of her nostrils with every exhale.*

*He was kissing her neck sloppily as he crushed her spine into the dirt and rocks, and she kept herself from retching by staring up at the treetops. It was dark down there on the ground, but the late afternoon autumn sky was brilliant blue and cloudless, as though everything was alright everywhere else.*

*Gregory raised up onto his knees and blocked her view of the real world. He looked off to the left and smiled.*

*"You want some?" he asked.*

Maggie bolted upright in her bed and heard Coco whimper softly beside her. She looked down at her, and let go of the handful of fur.

She grabbed her .45 and her phone from the nightstand, and with Coco at her heels, she slipped down the hall and cracked Sky's door open and made sure she was asleep. Then she stopped in Kyle's open doorway, soothed just a little by the sound of him softly snoring.

She walked into the kitchen, turned on the tap, and stuck her wrists under the flow.

Maggie had had the same dreams and the same flashbacks over and over for more than twenty years. Although her waking memory of the event was spotty, never, not once, had she ever remembered or dreamt that someone else had been there that day.

She rubbed a little water over her throat and face, then she turned off the faucet and stared past her reflection in the black window.

She tried to rationalize that it had just been a dream, an only partially real one, and that no one else had been there in the woods. But the moment she'd seen it, she'd known it was true.

Maggie looked down at her cell phone to check the time. It was just after 5:30. She flipped the phone open and speed-dialed her Dad. He'd never slept past five in his life.

"Hey, Sunshine," he answered quietly.

"Hey, Daddy," she said, willing her voice steady. "Are you going out this morning?"

"Yeah. Come on."

# CHAPTER
# SEVEN

Less than thirty minutes later, Maggie parked her Jeep at the Scipio Marina, grabbed her coffee from the console, and headed down the dock. Gray already had the engine going on his oyster skiff, and was winding the stern line around his arm.

He looked up and smiled as she approached the boat.

"There's my girl," he said. "Grab those tarps on your way aboard."

Maggie picked up the gray tarps that Daddy liked to put over his lap when he was culling, then stepped aboard. Once her father had pulled forward a bit and the skiff had drifted from the dock, she pulled up and stowed the bright orange fenders and sat down across the wooden platform from Gray.

Without any further conversation, they were underway. Maggie took a deep, cleansing breath of brine, and sighed as the breeze kissed her face.

Ever since she was small, Maggie had loved going out to the oyster beds with her father. In her teens, it became her escape. For more than twenty years, any time she felt overwhelmed or upset, she'd go out onto the bay with Gray.

He had never asked what was wrong. He had known without her telling it that she just needed to be out on the bay with him, with no sounds but the occasional boat, the ever present gulls, the lap of a wave, and the wet thumping of a clump of oysters hitting the platform.

Sometimes Gray knew why she needed it, like the day after she'd figured out she wouldn't be able to pay for law school, or the day before she'd asked David to leave.

Sometimes she talked to him about what was wrong, but as good and as loving as his advice always was, it was secondary to the grounding that the bay provided. She never talked to him about Gregory Boudreaux. She'd never told anyone, not even David. Especially not David.

When she'd finally managed to walk out of the woods, to climb onto her bike and ride home, every part of her body swearing it was broken, she'd told her parents that she'd fallen down a bank. They had believed her.

When the nightmares started, she'd made up a dream in which a nameless woman chased her on the beach. It was the same dream she recounted to David after they got married. He never noticed that they happened mostly in November. The anniversary month was usually her worst, but the dreams gradually lessened, and she'd rarely had them anymore. Until now.

As her father motored out into the bay that was only knee deep on a tall man, Maggie bent her head back and let the salty, damp air wind its way into her nose and mouth and throat. When they were a good way out, Daddy pointed off the port side, and they watched two dolphins dance a welcome.

Once Daddy got to one of his favorite beds, cut the motor, and dropped the sea anchor, Maggie dragged her hand through the water and lifted it to her face.

For the next hour, Maggie watched the sky go from dark to orange to gray and then blue as the sun rose over Apalach to the east. She watched her father walk up and down the sideboards, maneuvering the tongs that were almost triple his height, with two long, rectangular baskets at the bottom. He would sift and touch along the bottom until he found a good clump, then move the tongs like giant chopsticks, closing the baskets together.

He'd dump the booty on the wooden platform in the center of the boat, then go back to searching the bottom while Maggie tossed out small crabs, rocks, and seaweed. Once the pile on the platform was of a decent size, Gray sat down across from Maggie, handed her a culling iron, and the two of them went to work separating oyster from rock and oyster from oyster, throwing back the ones that were smaller than three inches.

It was still early yet for some of the oystermen, but they could see a handful of skiffs scattered among the beds in the distance. Here, though, they were alone, and the only sounds were the flat pinging of the culling irons against rock and shell. Every now and then, Daddy made a remark about a particularly nice oyster, which went in the home bucket, while the rest went in the canvas bag.

Finally, they'd swept the silt and other debris from the platform, and Daddy pulled a quart of freshly-squeezed orange juice and two lemons out of his cooler. He laid them out on an old plastic tablecloth while Maggie rinsed her hands in the bay.

Within five minutes, Gray had two dozen oysters shucked, their top shells tossed back into the water. The first oysters were always the best that they'd collected thus far, and were always eaten with a little bit of reverence. Gray cut the lemons into quarters, opened the orange juice and set it down between them, then handed Maggie her first. When he'd taken his, they both squeezed just a little lemon over them, closed their eyes, then slowly took the oysters into their mouths.

The oyster was briny at first taste, then once she bit into it, it had a sweetness that reminded her of creamed corn. She chewed slowly, savoring it before she swallowed. When she opened her eyes, Gray nodded at her.

"Yep," he said, as he always did.

"Yes," she answered, as she always had.

They made a little small talk as they ate the rest of their oysters and washed them down with the juice, then they headed back to the marina so that Maggie could go to work.

As she watched the water sparkle alongside the skiff, Maggie wondered if this was what it was like for farmers. She wondered if they walked out onto land that their fathers and grandfathers had farmed, scooped up a handful of black, loamy dirt and put their noses in it to remind them of what was real, of what was always. To remind themselves of who they were.

⚓ ⚓ ⚓

Bennett Boudreaux sat at the round table in the kitchen, reading the paper, eating a slice of wheat toast, and drinking his third cup of chicory coffee.

Amelia was frying bacon on the cooktop that was built into the island, one hand on her hip and the other holding a spatula. The sun was just coming up good, and it shone through the twelve-pane windows and burst into star showers over her head, reflecting off of the bright copper pots that hung from a huge piece of driftwood Bennett had made into a pot rack.

Bennett liked eating breakfast in the kitchen, though his wife, and, when they were still home, the boys, had always taken their breakfast at the cherry table in the dining room. Bennett preferred to eat in here, with Amelia and her mother, Miss Evangeline. It scandalized his wife within an inch of her life, which made him enjoy it all the more.

"You gon' eat some bacon?" Amelia asked him without looking up from her skillet.

"Nope," Bennett told his paper.

"You gon' eat some eggs?"

"Nope."

"She gon' be upset, you don't eat."

"She'll manage to live another ninety years anyway."

Just then, the back door opened and Miss Evangeline's walker preceded her into the kitchen.

"Mornin', Mama," Amelia said.

"Mornin', baby," Miss Evangeline answered, her voice like yellowed rice paper.

"Morning, Miss Evangeline," Boudreaux said.

"So you say," she said back.

Bennett stood and pulled back the chair across from his place, watched her make her way to the table.

Miss Evangeline was more than ninety years old and she looked every hour of it. She stood just under five feet tall, and her light-colored skin grasped her bones with no apparent flesh between the two. She wore her usual flowered house dress and straw slippers, and her shoes made sounds like sandpaper on wood as she slowly made her way to the table.

Miss Evangeline had been his father's housekeeper, but she might as well have been Bennett's nanny. His mother had been "delicate" and died when he was seven. His father had been too busy raising a business to raise a son. His father had left Miss Evangeline behind when he'd moved to Apalach, but when Bennett had finished college and started his business in Houma, he'd hired both her and Amelia. Now they were all here.

Amelia's job was to cook and clean and take care of her mother. Miss Evangeline's job didn't exist anymore, but she did it anyway.

Once she was abreast of him, Boudreaux leaned down and kissed both of her papery cheeks, then walked back to his seat.

Miss Evangeline slowly made what added up to a seven-point landing in her chair, and Boudreaux sat back down.

Amelia stepped away from her stove long enough to bring her mother a cup of tea. Boudreaux went back to his paper. Once settled, Miss Evangeline gingerly took a sip of the tea and then peered across the table, her eyes magnified behind her glasses.

"What in the papers today?" she asked.

Boudreaux looked at her over the top of the paper, then turned the page.

"Tropical Storm Claudette's not coming, Save the River's having a pancake fundraiser, and we're thanking everybody for their condolences on the halfwit."

"You don't keep talking ill of the dead. It's bad juju." Her hand trembled as she put the cup back in its saucer.

"Juju doesn't get Roman Catholics, Miss Evangeline; karma does."

She pointed a bent finger at him, the nail long and yellowed.

"Juju gets what it gets."

Boudreaux winked at her over the paper. "You keep trying to scare me with your voodoo and I'm gonna yank those tennis balls off your walker."

"Go on sass me, Mr. Benny. Sass me some more and I pass you a slap."

Amelia brought a plate of eggs and bacon to the table and set it down in front of her mother. The old woman looked at the plate, then looked over at the kitchen island.

"Where his food is?"

"He said he don't want anything," Amelia said, taking the skillet to the sink.

Miss Evangeline turned her gaze back to Boudreaux. She sat there a good minute, glaring at the newspaper in front of his face.

"Stop staring at me," he said pleasantly.

"Man 'sposed to eat."

"I eat."

"Mama, go on eat your breakfast," Amelia said from the sink. "I got to pass the mop before herself come down."

"Don't worry about her, Amelia," Boudreaux said. "She'll be down late. She's got several new black ensembles to try on before she decides what she's wearing to the funeral."

"I laid out your suit," Amelia said.

"Thank you. I saw that it was appropriately mournful."

Amelia grunted, then headed out of the kitchen.

Miss Evangeline put a morsel of scrambled egg into her mouth and chewed it as best she could while she stared across the table. After a minute, Boudreaux put the paper down.

"What?" he asked.

"Juju."

"Juju's what got Gregory, Miss Evangeline, and I'd say it was about time."

"Watch your mouth," she said, pointing her fork at him.

"He didn't become a better person because he's dead, old woman. We're not going to pretend he was a saint now."

"All the same, you got to hold your tongue."

"I did, Miss Evangeline," Boudreaux said. "As you well know. Now let's get the little piece of garbage into the ground and be done with it."

"I gon' pray for you, then I gon' come over there and snatch you up."

Boudreaux drank the last of his coffee, put the cup down, and smiled.

"I'll be at the office by the time you make it over here."

CHAPTER

# EIGHT

**S**o what do we know?" Wyatt asked.

He was sitting in the metal chair in Maggie's office, resting one foot on the opposite knee and tapping a pen against the legal pad in his lap. Maggie was sitting on the edge of her desk and Lt. James Caulfield, from the Narcotics Division, sat at the other desk a few feet away.

"Not much, yet," said Maggie. "All Grace knows is that this deal is supposed to involve more product than he usually handles."

"Well, Joey Truman is strictly small time," James said. "He's Alessi's lap dog and he's never done anything without him. Barone, he's a different fish. He's from Gainesville. Two priors for aggravated assault and he got busted in 2002 for possession with intent. No indictment. Search and seizure issues."

"What did we bust Alessi with in '07?" Wyatt asked.

James flipped through a file on the desk in front of him.

"A little over two kilos," Maggie answered. "Nothing since he got out in 2012."

"What we need is the cooking facility and we just can't get it," James said. "Aside from the fact that they move those things around all the time, as far as we know, Alessi never goes there. We surveilled him for a while last year, but came up empty. We know he's setting things up with his cronies and one of the cronies is going back and forth to the lab, but we don't have the manpower to tail every of one his associates."

"Let's say we got him with just two kilos or so this time around," Maggie said. "What kind of time might he be looking at?"

"I don't know." James shook his head and ran a hand through his sandy, thinning hair. "He'll be classified a habitual felony offender. He's got that second-degree felony arrest for coke back in...'09? He'll be gone for a while."

"Well, as far as this girl is concerned, the more immediate question is will he get bail," Wyatt said. "Did you talk to her about that, Maggie?"

"No, I didn't want to scare her," Maggie said. "I'm going to bring it up to the ASA. Honestly, if he can't give me at least some assurance that Alessi won't get bail awaiting trial, I don't want her to do this."

"Well, but that's not your choice," James said with a shrug. "She'll be coming to you with knowledge of felony activity."

"I know," Maggie said. "But she has nowhere to go."

Wyatt threw his pen down on her desk. "These lost kids," he snapped. "I don't know how you people raise teenagers without taking some kind of medication."

They all sighed and sat silent for a moment, then Wyatt looked at his watch.

"Did she tell you when she'd be calling?" he asked.

"No. Just some time today," Maggie said.

"Well, Greggs, Peterson, and Lowicki are on duty tomorrow night and I've got Paulsen and Messer on stand-by," James said. "We'll get with SWAT once we know something definite, get some additional officers from PD, too."

"Don't forget me," Wyatt said.

"I want to go, too," Maggie said.

"You're not narcotics anymore," Wyatt said shortly.

"You're not narcotics, either," Maggie answered.

"I'm the Sheriff; I get to be whatever I want."

"And she's my informant," Maggie said.

Wyatt sighed and stood up, stretched his impossibly long legs. "We can argue about this in the car," he said. "Let's go talk to the ASA."

"Let me know what's going on," James said as he got up and headed for the door.

"I can go myself," Maggie said, once he'd left.

"Well, you could, but since he has an appointment with *me*, he wouldn't be available for *you*." Wyatt stopped in her doorway and turned on her as she stumbled just short of running into his chest. "Besides, I'm planning on stopping at the soda fountain after and if you want ice cream, you will have to come with me."

"Sometimes, I'm not even sure you're a grown-up," Maggie said.

"I might be able to help you with that," he said, and walked out the door.

⚓  ⚓  ⚓

"I didn't try this case, but I remember it," Assistant State's Attorney Patrick Boudreaux said. "And, of course, I'm familiar with Alessi." He closed the manila file they'd brought him and leaned his elbows on his desk and folded his hands.

"So what is it that you need from me at this point?" he asked them.

Wyatt opened his mouth, but Maggie spoke first.

"I need to be able to give this girl assurance that her name's going to be left out of it."

Patrick shrugged his shoulders in his hundred-dollar shirt and Maggie thought about punching him. She only knew him in the course of work, but she'd never liked him. His dark hair was too perfect, his manicure too shiny, and he walked with the loose-limbed gait of a man convinced of his own attractiveness but trying to give the impression he never thought about it.

Additionally, Maggie found the persistence with which he pursued convictions conveniently inconsistent.

"If you bust these guys in the middle of a transaction, or even just holding that much meth, they're going to go down with minimal testimony," Boudreaux said. "She's an informant. I see no reason to bring her into it."

"What about bail?" Wyatt asked. "Any chance you can keep him locked up until trial?"

Patrick spread his palms and sighed, but a little too cheerfully for Maggie's taste.

"Depends on the judge. If we get Carson or Newell, bail denied. If we get Anderson or *Ms.* Rillette it could go either way. But if I was his attorney, I'd advise him to plead guilty. In any event, most likely, he'll be remanded to County until his trial."

"Most likely," Maggie repeated.

"Right," Patrick said, as though to a child.

Wyatt stood up and Patrick handed him the file.

"Just keep me apprised and I'll see what I can do," Patrick said. "Meanwhile, I have a funeral to attend, unfortunately."

They both looked at Maggie, who remained seated. She thought for a moment that it was just possible that Bennett Boudreaux would have made a better State's Attorney than his son did.

"This girl's taking a huge risk," she said.

Patrick tossed her a condescending look. "I'd say she took that risk when she hooked up with him, didn't she?"

Maggie opened her mouth to answer, but Wyatt put a hand on her shoulder.

"Well, Lt. Redmond and I have another appointment, so one of us will get back to you as soon as we hear something," Wyatt said.

"I'll talk to you then, Sheriff Hamilton."

Maggie got up and nodded at Patrick as she followed Wyatt out.

"Mr. Boudreaux," she said.

"Maggie," he replied.

⚓  ⚓  ⚓

The Old Time Soda Fountain was located on a quaint block downtown, surrounded by gift shops, small art galleries, and seafood restaurants. Open since 1905, it had been Apalach's favorite spot for ice cream for generations. Maggie and her Mom had come in for root beer floats or cherry Cokes many Saturdays when Maggie was young, and now Maggie brought her kids. Unless they were lactose-intolerant, every kid in Apalachicola had spent a good amount of time sitting at the old counter and shoveling in banana splits.

Wyatt and Maggie sat on one of the white benches outside. Wyatt had a double waffle cone, coffee and butter pecan. Maggie had a single scoop of pineapple sherbet.

"It must really rust Boudreaux's bucket that his firstborn is such a Ken doll," Wyatt said.

Maggie smiled at him and watched in wonder as he took a giant bite of his ice cream.

"You think he's gay?" Wyatt asked.

"How would I know? Who cares?"

"Well, if he's not, he should be."

Maggie took a bite of her ice cream.

"I've always heard that he's quite the ladies' man," she said.

"Yeah, well you've heard that about me, too and that's not true, either."

Maggie gave him a look, which he ignored.

"So, when we get back to the office, do some more looking at Barone. Let's see exactly who we're dealing with. Of course, we have no idea yet who *they're* dealing with."

"Okay," Maggie said, looking at her watch. It was almost three.

Wyatt wiped his mouth with his napkin and stared at Maggie.

"You're not done? Come on, we gotta go. I've got a meeting at four."

Maggie followed Wyatt to his cruiser and climbed into the passenger seat. Wyatt watched her trying to buckle herself in with one hand while she held her cone in the other.

"Oh, for crying out loud," he said.

He leaned over her and pushed her seat belt in. She wasn't sure, but this might have been the closest they'd ever been physically. He smelled of salt and sun, coffee and Nautilus. She liked it, then felt bad for that.

He straightened up and started the cruiser, turned on the blessed AC.

"Don't drip all over the seat; the county gets pissy."

"I'm not," she snapped.

They drove in silence for a few minutes, until they were on the bridge back to Eastpoint.

"So what are you doing later?" he asked her casually.

"Uh, my parents are having us over for barbecue and Scrabble. They just finished building a deck."

"That sounds fun," he said and she heard no sarcasm in his voice.

"What are you doing?"

"Not much," he said. "I might go get a bite to eat. Or maybe just go home and watch baseball. The Bucs are playing, bless their hearts."

"Why don't you come with us?"

Maggie had said it before she'd thought it, and she was more surprised by the invitation than he was.

"To your Mom and Dad's?"

"Well, yeah," she said. "I mean, it's no big deal. It's not like I'm bringing you home to talk to my Dad."

"I talk to your Dad all the time."

That was true. Wyatt and Gray knew each other from plenty of Christmas parties and local events, and had even gone fishing once or twice.

"You know what I mean," Maggie said.

"What you meant is neither here nor there," he said. "I'd love to come, if you're sure they won't mind."

"No, they'll be glad I asked. They like you."

"I'm very likable," he said with a grin. "Are you sure they'll have enough food?"

"For you? No, I'm not sure. You'd better stop and pick up some sandwiches or something."

He gave her a look. "Do *you* have to come?"

CHAPTER

# NINE

**B**ennett Boudreaux stood patiently near the flower-covered casket that was poised above the open grave. His face was perfectly sincere and solemn as he accepted handshakes, pats on the back and the occasional squeeze of his shoulder from the line of people that passed in front of the family.

To his left was his wife, Lily, occasionally dabbing at her eyeliner with one of his handkerchiefs. He wondered if it was good for her to be out in direct sunlight for so long. It seemed to him that it might melt or otherwise damage the Botox or seahorse blood or whatever it was she had injected into her face on a regular basis. He also wondered how much sense it made to pay thousands of dollars to preserve something that wasn't that pleasing to begin with.

His younger son, Craig, stood on the other side of Lily, with his petite, blonde wife Ellie and their three kids. Patrick stood on Bennett's right, checking his cell phone between condolences. It irritated Bennett; appearances were everything, and Patrick could at least give the appearance of having no place more important to be.

As Bennett shook the hand of his accountant and nodded his thanks, he noticed Brandon Wilmette a few people down, at the end of the line. Bennett managed not to grimace.

Brandon was more commonly known as Sport, so named because the only thing he'd ever been good at was athletics. He was one of Gregory's few close friends and Bennett had barely tolerated him for years. He and Gregory had met as freshmen at Tulane and Gregory had brought him home for most vacations and holidays throughout their unremarkable educations.

Sport was a high-bred hanger on and parasite, much like Gregory had been. Always another great opportunity to make money, always another excuse for why it went wrong. He'd talked Gregory into investing in several doomed endeavors, which was part of the reason why Gregory had depended on Bennett for his livelihood, even at the age of forty.

Sport shook Patrick's hand and exchanged a few words, then he waited for just a moment after the last guest had moved on, approached Bennett and held out his hand. Bennett found his white tee shirt and green Miami Vice suit inappropriate to both the occasion and the century.

"Mr. Boudreaux, sir. I'm really sorry about Gregory."

Bennett shook the man's hand.

"Thank you, Sport. It's good to see you," Bennett lied.

"When Craig called me in Atlanta...well, I got down here as soon as I could," Sport said.

Bennett nodded again and wished him away. Sport glanced over at the rest of the family. Patrick had joined Craig and his family, and Lily was busy talking with the accountant's pasty wife.

Sport leaned in to Bennett and spoke just above a whisper. "Mr. Boudreaux, I really need to speak with you. It's important."

"Well, we're having guests over to the house," Bennett said. "You're welcome to join us."

"I think we should speak privately, sir," Sport said. "It's about Gregory."

Bennett regarded him for a moment, then gently pulled him a few feet away from the others.

"What's on your mind, son?"

"Well, I really think we should talk when we have a little more time and privacy, sir."

He waited for Bennett to respond, but Bennett seemed to be waiting for an explanation. Sport glanced over at the others to make sure no one was listening, then spoke again in a whisper.

"It's about how he died," he said. "And maybe why."

"He killed himself, son. Gregory had a lot of problems."

"Maybe," Sport answered. "But I have some other ideas. Maybe some things you should know."

Bennett thought a minute, then nodded.

"Alright. I'm going to be tied up the rest of the day and most of tomorrow. I'll be going into the office tomorrow evening to do some catching up. Will you still be in town?"

"I can be," Sport answered.

"Then why don't you come by around seven or so?"

"Thank you, sir," Sport said, shaking his hand again. "I'll see you then."

Bennett nodded and watched Sport stop to say a few words to the rest of the family. Bennett couldn't help feeling, as he watched Sport walk away, that he had been burdened with more than his fair share of dumbasses.

⚓ ⚓ ⚓

Maggie's parents had been fortunate to buy their property, on Hwy 98 just where it rolled into the west side of town, back when it was relatively cheap. It wasn't the nicest stretch of road, a mixture of simple houses and commercial buildings, but Maggie's folks had their beloved bay in back and they never spent much time in the front yard anyway. Last year, they'd thrown a big party to celebrate paying off their mortgage.

Tonight, Gray had done himself proud, grilling up some fine T-bone steaks and fresh Florida corn, which Georgia had supplemented with some salad and her famous mushroom rice. Everyone sat around the redwood picnic table on Gray and Georgia's new deck, which overlooked the back yard and, beyond it, the bay.

The evening had been perfect for an outdoor meal. The rain that had threatened earlier had never materialized, and now, as the sun set over the water, there was just enough breeze to keep the mosquitoes away.

Maggie and the kids sat on one side of the table, her parents and Wyatt on the other. Several times during the meal, Maggie had found herself looking at Wyatt across from her and thinking that he looked right at home with the people she loved most in the world. It had unsettled her, but comforted her at the same time somehow.

"Y'all, this was the best meal I've had in a long time," Wyatt said. "Thank you for having me."

"Our pleasure, Wyatt," Gray said. "It's nice to have company."

"I enjoy feeding people that like to eat," Georgia added.

"Well, then you must be beside yourself tonight," Wyatt said.

"Sunshine, I think it's about that time, don't you?" Gray asked.

"Ugh." Sky rolled her eyes, but she was grinning.

Gray took a pull on his beer and winked at Maggie. "Wyatt, what is your position on Scrabble?"

"I'm in favor of it," Wyatt answered. "Good game."

"You're doomed," Maggie said, smiling. "Scrabble isn't a game around here; it's serious business."

"You have time to play a game, Wyatt?" Gray asked.

"Sure."

"How about you, Squirt?"

Sky made a face at her grandfather, then grinned. "School just got out. Who wants to spend two hours in English class?"

"Can we play Minecraft in the den?" Kyle piped up.

"Go on," Gray answered. "After you help your Grandma clear the table."

The kids got up and started stacking plates.

"Just remember that you were warned, Wyatt," Maggie said.

"Ah, I'm not scared. I know lots of words."

Georgia got up and started clearing the table. "Well, I play for kicks, but Maggie and Gray, they play for keeps."

"Yeah, but Dad's game has really slipped since he lost his lucky lung," Maggie said.

Gray grinned as he got up from his chair.

"Maggie chooses to play a psychological game to try to gain some advantage," he said. "It makes her feel more formidable."

"Well, this should be fun," Wyatt said as he stood up.

⚓   ⚓   ⚓

While Wyatt and Gray finished their beers on the deck and cleaned the grill, Maggie helped her mother rinse the dishes and load them into the dishwasher.

Georgia looked out the window at the men on the deck.

"I'm glad you brought him with you tonight, honey," she said.

"Me, too. I think he gets lonely," Maggie answered.

"So do you."

Maggie focused on scraping salad scraps into the trash. "I have the kids. And you guys."

"It's not the same," her mother said.

"It is what it is," Maggie said with a shrug.

They worked without speaking for a moment, the running water and the rattle of dishes and utensils all that broke the silence.

"We miss David, too," Georgia finally said.

Maggie swallowed hard and nodded.

Georgia looked back out to the deck, where Wyatt and Gray were laughing about something.

"But he's a good man," Georgia said. "And I think he cares about you."

Maggie glanced out the window, too.

"I'm not sure. I mean, we're friends, and we do have this flirtation thing going on, but I don't know how to read other men. There's always just been David."

"Well, I read him just fine," Georgia said. "He cares. And I approve."

Maggie leaned a hip against the counter and fiddled with the dishcloth in her hand.

"I don't know, Mom. Somehow, it still feels like it would be cheating. David still loves me. And I still love him, deeply, but I can never be *in* love with him again."

Georgia reached over and tucked a strand of Maggie's hair behind her ear. "I know. Y'all were peas in a pod since you were ten years old. That's never really going to go away."

"All I ever wanted was to have what you and Daddy have," Maggie said. "I thought we had that."

"Listen, honey. Your daddy and I have been blessed, but we've had our problems, too. Especially in the beginning. We almost didn't even get married."

"Really? Why?"

"Just typical stuff, but that's a story for another time," Georgia said, waving her off. "But we got a second chance, and I think you have a second chance, too. Y'all should go have a cocktail or something after the game."

"We can't exactly do that, Mom. He's my boss, remember?"

"Well, then just go somewhere private. With the kids spending the night, it's a perfect opportunity to be alone, just the two of you."

"For what?"

"To just spend some time. I'm not telling you to sleep with him, Maggie," Georgia said, laughing.

"Oh, Mom!" Maggie threw the towel over her face. "Go away."

⚓   ⚓   ⚓

The Scrabble game was close, intense and taken very seriously, as per usual. Maggie lost by more than a hundred points, which both men remarked upon with some glee. Maggie blamed her poor performance on the fact that Wyatt stared at her frequently. When she'd catch him at it, he didn't bother giving her one of his goofy grins. It made her extremely nervous. She wondered why she had no trouble tackling a wife-beater or taking a punch, but having Wyatt stare at her made her feel like a six-year old girl.

For his part, Wyatt gained considerable respect from Gray by losing to the older man by just a few points. He blamed shrapnel in his knee, but couldn't be too specific about where he got it.

While Wyatt said his goodnights to her parents, Maggie went into the den to say goodbye to the kids.

Kyle was deeply involved in Minecraft, but Sky had apparently abandoned the game. She was lying on the couch, texting her friends, with her legs slung across her little brother's lap.

"I'm leaving, you guys," Maggie said.

Both of the kids looked up from their respective screens.

"Did you lose again?" Kyle asked.

"Yeah," Maggie answered, then kissed the top of his head. "Be good for Grandma and Granddad, okay?"

"I will. Did you pack Stitch?" Kyle was growing up, but he still slept with his favorite stuffed animal.

"I did. I love you, you know."

"I love you more," Kyle answered.

"Oh, here we go," Sky said.

"I love you ten times that," Maggie said.

"I love you infinity times everything you say after this," Kyle said. "Is Wyatt leaving, too?"

"Yeah," Maggie said.

"Oh, really?" Sky said, grinning.

"Hush." Maggie leaned over and kissed her daughter's forehead.

"I like him," Kyle said.

"Good. He's a nice guy."

"And?" Sky asked.

"And nothing. He's a great guy."

"You know, Mom, it's okay to be happy," Sky answered.

"I am happy, nitwit."

"You know what I mean. If you and Dad aren't going to be together, then it's okay to move on."

"Well, I'm not...we're not dating or anything."

"Well, you should be. He's freakin' hot for an old guy."

Maggie laughed and ran a hand through her daughter's hair. "He's forty-eight."

"Yeah, like I said. But, dude. Hot, right?"

"Yeah, kinda," Maggie said, trying not to smile much.

"Do you still love Daddy?" Kyle asked quietly, and, at that moment, he'd never looked more like David. Maggie swallowed and nodded.

"I'll always love your Dad," she said.

"But different?"

"Yeah, but different, buddy."

Kyle nodded and his expression made him seem much older than he was. "Yeah."

⚓ ⚓ ⚓

Gray followed Wyatt out to the front steps.

"Thanks again, Gray," Wyatt said. "This was nice."

"Any time, son. We enjoyed having you," Gray said.

They both looked out toward Hwy 98, as a couple of cars passed by, their headlights sweeping the porch.

"You know, no matter how old your daughter gets, or how likable her companions, you still have the same instincts."

Wyatt nodded.

"So, I'm obligated to say that I see how you look at Maggie and I know how things are," Gray continued.

"Well, we haven't exactly gone on a date or anything, sir. That's a little complicated, what with the jobs."

Gray nodded. "I guess that would be true. But I see how she looks at you, too, and I don't doubt that you'll find a way around those complications. I think you're a good man, Wyatt, and I'd like to see her happy again."

Wyatt nodded. "Yes, sir."

"I'll just say this. You might be the Sheriff and you might have fifty pounds on me, but I will knock your ass out if you're careless with my girl."

"Duly noted, sir," Wyatt said, smiling. "And I like you all the more for it."

"Good enough," Gray said and shook Wyatt's hand as Maggie came out the front door.

"What are y'all doing?" she asked as she came alongside her dad.

"Guy stuff," her father said.

"What kind of guy stuff?"

"The kind that's not girl stuff," Wyatt said. "C'mon, let's let your Dad recover from kicking my butt at Scrabble."

Maggie gave her Dad a suspicious look as Wyatt headed for the driveway where their cars were parked.

"Just fishing stories," Gray said as he hugged Maggie. "Goodnight, Sunshine."

"Night, Daddy, thank you," Maggie said, then headed after Wyatt.

Gray went inside and turned off the porch light. Wyatt was leaning against the hood of his pickup, playing with his keys. Maggie didn't know whether to go over there or not, or what she'd do when she got there, so she walked to her car and put her hands on her own hood. They just looked at each other for a minute and Maggie found herself missing Wyatt's usual jocularity.

"That was nice. I'm glad you enjoyed it." Maggie said finally.

"I did. A lot."

He kept staring at her, without smiling, and Maggie spoke just to break the silence.

"My Mom told me I should ask you out for a drink or something," she said, then tried to laugh.

"I'd go."

Maggie shrugged. "But it wouldn't look good, us out drinking together."

"No."

Maggie looked at the keys in her hand for a minute.

"But...do you want to come sit on my deck, have a glass of wine or something?"

Wyatt finally smiled. "Yep."

⚓    ⚓    ⚓

Wyatt had never been to Maggie's home, even when she'd still been married. He followed her there and was immediately set upon by Stoopid, who never slept and felt obliged to flap and posture at every visitor.

Once the rooster had been called off, Coco stepped in to appraise the situation. Maggie was impressed that Coco seemed to like Wyatt almost immediately, and the dog stayed right behind him as he wandered around.

While Maggie dug out an old bottle of Muscadine wine and a couple of glasses in the kitchen, Wyatt looked at the family pictures on the wall and the old life preserver, culling iron, and oar that had been her grandfather's.

"This is really nice," Wyatt called from the living room.

"Thanks," Maggie answered. "My Grandpa built this house."

"Secluded."

"Yes."

"A security system would be nice," he mentioned.

Maggie walked into the living room. Wyatt was bent over, inspecting her deadbolt.

"I have Coco," she said.

Wyatt stood up and walked over to Maggie, Coco on his trail.

"I like Coco. But a security system would be nice."

"I've also got my .45, my grandfather's .38 is on top of the fridge, and there's a Mossberg 500 on the shelf in the closet."

Wyatt took the glass of wine she held out. "No tripwires?"

"Stoopid's my tripwire. You want to go out on the deck?"

"Sure."

Maggie led the way through the sliding door in the living room and they sat down on the back deck. It was a half moon, and the moonlight made the river sparkle. Coco sat down next to Maggie and smiled over at Wyatt.

They sipped their wine without speaking for a moment; the frogs and crickets carried the conversation. Maggie became uncomfortable with the silence fairly quickly. She was used to easy repartee with Wyatt.

"I'm a little worried that Grace hasn't called," she said.

Wyatt looked at his watch. "It's only nine. Maybe she still will."

Maggie nodded. They looked at each other for a minute, until she had to look down at her wine.

"Let's not talk about work," Wyatt said.

"Okay." Maggie smiled self-consciously. "What should we talk about?"

"Well, why don't we get a few things out on the table before your nerves are shot."

"My nerves are fine," she said weakly.

"No, they're not," he answered. "You look like you're gonna throw yourself off the deck."

Maggie smiled. "I'm sorry, I'm just not used to this. It feels foreign, you being here."

"Do you want me to go?"

"No."

"But you're not sure what we're doing."

"No."

Wyatt nodded. "Let me see if I can help you out a little." He leaned his elbows on his knees. "I know we joke around about me and other women, but most of it's just kidding around."

"You're a single guy. You're supposed to date."

"It's nice to have somebody to see a movie with or go out for dinner, but that's all it is," Wyatt said. "I'll be honest. I was kind of a dog before I met Lily, but I haven't been with a woman since."

Maggie nodded, unsure what she should say.

"I don't like dating. I liked being married," Wyatt said. "I liked everything about it."

"She must have been something," Maggie offered.

"She was. For fifteen years, I was a very happy guy."

Coco suddenly ran to the railing and peered out at the dark woods. Wyatt and Maggie both stood up to look. On a scrub pine ten feet away, a possum stared at them, his eyes glowing red. Wyatt leaned back against the rail and Maggie picked her wine up from the table and took a healthy swallow.

"Here's the thing. I'm old enough and smart enough that when I find someone I can be that happy with again, I'm just gonna marry her. I don't want to piss around for a few years. I like having someone know what I'm thinking just by looking at me. I like knowing the smell of her hair by heart. I like the routines and the predictability and the comfortable silences. And I like sleeping with the same woman every night."

Maggie was taken aback, by both Wyatt's directness and the reminders of what she'd had with David. The juxtaposition made it hard for her to know what to say.

"I like that," she said anyway.

"Good." Wyatt set his glass down on the rail and folded his arms across his chest. "I know we're just kind of dancing around this whole idea of following up on this attraction—I assume it's actually mutual?"

Maggie nodded.

"So, we're pondering that and we haven't as yet actually done anything about it, but now you know what I would hope to get out of it."

"Okay."

"Of course, you've got that on the one hand and, on the other, there's the fact of our jobs and that it's against department policy for us to be involved, and I'm kind of hoping for early retirement in two years."

Maggie wanted to say something relevant and intelligent, but they'd gone from harmless flirtation to the ramifications of a serious relationship in the course of a day, and she was scrambling to find some footing.

"You should consider, too, while you're weighing things, that I'm quite an impressive kisser."

She was relieved to see his familiar, dimpled smile and she laughed.

"Is that so?" she asked.

"Possibly without peer."

Maggie felt better and worse simultaneously. The lighthearted remark relaxed her, but the thought of kissing Wyatt put all kinds of knots in her.

They looked at each other a moment and their smiles faded.

"Are you considering that? Because I'm thinking about coming over there," Wyatt said.

"Okay," Maggie answered stupidly.

Wyatt stepped away from the railing and set his glass down on the table. Just then, Coco tore across the deck and around to the front, and they heard her tags and toenails as she ran down the stairs. A moment later, a vehicle pulled into the gravel out front.

The fact that Coco didn't bark was a clue, but Maggie didn't need one. She knew the sound of David's Toyota truck.

She put down her wine and followed Wyatt around to the front. They stood near the top of the stairs as David got out of the truck. Wyatt turned to Maggie.

"And now we're filming a Lifetime movie," he said.

David knelt down and rubbed Coco, who was falling apart at his feet, then stood and smiled up at Maggie and Wyatt.

"Hey guys," he said. "I'm sorry, is this a bad time?"

"No, I was just about to head home," Wyatt said, and started down the stairs. He stopped and turned back to Maggie. "We'll talk later about that evidence, Maggie. I think you'll find it convincing."

"Okay," Maggie managed. "I'll see you tomorrow."

Wyatt continued down the stairs. "If you hear from her, call me."

"I will." Maggie followed Wyatt down to the driveway, where he stuck a hand out to David.

"How are ya, David?"

"Good, Wyatt. You?"

"Hanging in there," Wyatt said as they shook.

"Well, keep safe."

"You, too." Wyatt raised a hand over his head to Maggie and walked to his truck. He opened his door and glanced back at her, then got in and drove away, leaving Maggie and David standing in the yard.

Maggie watched Wyatt pull onto the dirt drive, then looked at the man who used to be her husband. He looked good, and so familiar. His glossy, black hair was just below the collar of the flannel shirt he wore open over a tee shirt. He would look much younger without the closely-trimmed beard. He was much shorter and slighter than Wyatt, only five-ten and athletically slim.

Maggie looked at him as he stood there with his hands in his jeans pockets, and her son's big, pretty eyes looked back at her.

"I'm sorry, babe," he said. "Sky and I were texting today and she said they were spending the night with your folks. I figured you were alone."

"It was just work," Maggie said.

He half-smiled at her and shook his head just once. "No, it wasn't. But you have the right, Maggie."

Maggie sighed. "Well, we were just talking."

"I'm sorry I barged in. Mostly sorry."

He took his hands out of his pockets and walked up, put his arms around her.

"How are you?" he asked as she hugged him back.

"I'm okay. How are you?"

He stood back, scratched Coco on the neck.

"I'm good. I just got back from two weeks in Mobile, wanted to check on you."

"What were you doing in Mobile?" she asked.

"I helped a guy rebuild the engine on his shrimp boat," David said. "He's gonna give me a good deal on a boat in return."

"You're buying a boat?" Maggie asked, surprised.

"Well, yeah. I'm not living on that houseboat just 'cause I'm cheap," he said, almost shyly. "I'm saving up to pay cash this time."

"That's good, David. I'm glad, really."

David nodded at her. "You look tired, babe. Are you sleeping?"

"Yeah. I've just been working a lot."

"I heard about Gregory Boudreaux. That must have sucked."

Maggie kept from rubbing her arms by sheer force of will.

"Yeah. Well."

"I guess I feel sorry for the guy, but he was kind of an ass. I've seen him at Papa Joe's a few times, hammered out of his mind."

Maggie avoided saying anything else by squatting down and scratching Coco. David watched her for a minute.

"Hey," he said quietly. She looked up at him. "I'm buying that boat."

"You should," she said.

"You're trying to look encouraging, but I see you chewing on your lip." He smiled and shrugged. "Hey, they're gonna make pot legal, anyway."

Maggie didn't want to answer the question he was thinking. She knew they'd never get back together, even if he did stop running pot.

"Do you know Richard Alessi?" she asked.

"I don't deal with meth heads, Maggie, you know that."

"But you know who he is."

"Yeah, I know who he is. But I told you, I don't even hang around with the pot people. Why are you asking about Alessi?"

Maggie stood up and shrugged. "I'm just working on something."

"He's a freak, babe. You need to stay away from him," David said. "And he needs to stay far away from you."

"It's okay," she said.

Suddenly, she was reminded of the time they'd gone to see *Silence of the Lambs,* when they were in sixth grade. They were supposed to be seeing *Point Break*, but snuck in to the R-rated movie instead. It had scared the crap out of Maggie, but she'd refused to leave out of pride. Through all of the frightening scenes, David had tucked her face into his shoulder and put his arms around her, and it had had nothing to do with feeling her up or looking cool. She'd known then that he would always make her feel safe, that he would always be her sanctuary. She'd thought she'd known it, anyway.

An unexpected tear crept down her cheek. David stepped close and took her face in his hands, tilted it up to look at him.

"Hey."

"I'm just tired. I need to go in," she said.

"You're not all by yourself, Maggie," he said. "Wyatt's got your back, you've got your folks."

Maggie stared into his eyes, eyes she could still draw perfectly from memory, and nodded.

"And you've got me," he said. "In one form or another, it's always us. Always has been."

Maggie put her hands on his and took them away from her face, kissed his palm and let them go.

"I know."

David kissed her forehead.

"I love you, babe."

"I love you, too."

She watched him walk to his truck, Coco right on his heels. He leaned down and rubbed the dog's neck. "Love you, Coco. Go to Mama."

Coco ran back to Maggie, and David waved and got into his truck. Maggie turned and walked away, feeling like someone had been punching her in the chest all day long. She was pretty sure that she'd never be able to be with David again, boat or no boat, pot or no pot. But, God help her, he was still the best friend she'd ever had.

⚓ ⚓ ⚓

Maggie had just fallen asleep when her cell phone woke her. She reached over and picked it up, recognized the number as Grace's.

"Grace," she said.

"Ms. Redmond, I'm really sorry it's so late, but this is the first chance I've had to call you." Grace's voice was hushed.

"It's okay," Maggie said, getting out of bed. Coco jumped down and followed her out of the room.

"They're meeting some guys out off of Burnt Bridge Road, out there in Tate's Hell? Ricky was talking to Joey about it over here at the house, then I heard him giving directions to somebody else on the phone."

Maggie grabbed a notepad and pen from the counter and sat down at the kitchen table. "Okay, do you know when?"

"Eleven o'clock tomorrow night. At some old lookout tower or something the rangers use."

Maggie scribbled on the pad.

"I didn't hear everything he said to the guy on the phone," Grace said. "But I know he said there was a turn-off, like an ATV trail, 1.4 miles in. I'm not sure if that was from Burnt Bridge or not, though. I never been out there."

"Okay, Grace. I'll find it. Do you know who's going to be there?"

"Not exactly. I know he will, and Joey and Gary. That might have been Gary he was talking to. But the guys they're meeting, I don't know anything about that."

"Okay," Maggie said, writing it down. "Where's Ricky now?"

"He went to get some beer."

"Do you what they're doing tomorrow, exactly?"

"They're selling these guys a bunch of crystal. Guys Ricky's never dealt with before. Ricky's real excited, but I think he's kind of nervous, too," Grace said. "Joey said something about ten keys and they were talking about what they were going to buy after they paid the guys that work in the lab."

Maggie did some quick math on the notepad. She'd been out of narcotics for five years, but she figured ten kilos was worth about six hundred thousand dollars on the market. Ricky was a wholesaler, but he was making some big money. A lot more than he was used to.

"Okay, Grace. I talked to the Assistant State's Attorney, and he's agreed that there's no reason to ask you to testify or anything if this goes to court. He's also fairly sure Richard won't get bail this time, but you need to think of somewhere to go if he does."

There was a long silence, with the exception of Grace's breathing.

"Grace?"

"I'm just gonna pray they don't give him bail."

"Listen to me. You call me or you call 911 the minute you even think you need to, do you understand?"

"If he gets out on bail, will you know right away?"

"I'll go to the bail hearing myself."

"You could call me right away and tell me? I could leave the phone on that day, you know?"

"Yes."

Maggie heard the girl take a deep breath and let it out quickly. "This is what I need to do," she said.

"Okay. Get off the phone and stash it, okay?"

"I am."

Maggie was going to say something reassuring, but Grace had hung up. She disconnected and speed-dialed Wyatt. He answered on the second ring.

"What's up?" he asked groggily.

"Grace called. They're meeting at eleven tomorrow night, out in Tate's Hell."

She heard a rustle of sheets or covers, and the sound of a mattress squeaking.

"Alright, I'll call James and we'll all sit down tomorrow morning. Eight o'clock."

"Okay."

There was a pause. Maggie wasn't sure what to say to fill it.

"Everything alright with David?" Wyatt asked, saving her the trouble. She heard him trying to sound casual.

"Yeah. He just stayed a few minutes. Checking on me."

"Well, we'll continue that conversation soon."

"Okay."

"Doors locked? Freaky rooster on duty?"

Maggie couldn't help smiling. "Everything's battened down, as usual."

"Good. Then get some sleep."

"Goodnight, Sheriff."

"Goodnight, Lieutenant."

CHAPTER

TEN

**E**veryone was piled into the conference room at the Sheriff's Department. Wyatt stood at one end of the long table, flanked by James from narcotics, and Frank Pittman, captain of the SWAT team.

Standing along both sides of the table with Maggie were five deputies from Narcotics, two SWAT guys, and four other deputies who just happened to be scheduled for duty later that night.

Capt. Pittman unrolled a large map, laid it down in front of Wyatt, and took out a pen.

"Here's the old ranger station here," he said, using the pen as a pointer. "It's no longer in use. Really more of a lookout than a station, not much bigger than a good deer stand. It's the only one even remotely close, according to the directions you got from your contact, so we're saying this is it."

He dragged the pen along a barely visible line that ran north and south a few hundred yards from the ranger station. "Right here, we've got an ATV trail that's currently closed because of downed trees. Access is from this road over here, about a quarter mile from the target location. I believe the trail your target's supposed to use is the one on the other side of the lookout. As you can see, it's right off Burnt Bridge Road, and you run about five hundred yards before you get to the location."

"So are we going in via this closed trail, then?" Wyatt asked.

"That's what I'm thinking, Sheriff. It means circling around the long way from town, but the likelihood of being spotted is minimal, I think."

Wyatt leaned over and peered at the map. There were a few trees penciled in to indicate woods between the closed trail and the lookout.

"What kind of cover are we going to get from these woods here?"

"None, unless you're sending some toddlers in. This is all new growth scrub pines, some no bigger around than my arm," Pittman said. "Most of these losers are totally fried in the head, but these guys actually picked a pretty decent spot. Very little cover, not a widely used area, and the lookout's called a lookout for a reason. It's on stilts, approximately twelve feet high. Good visibility all the way around, with a window here and one on the opposite wall here."

"So how are we working this, then?" Wyatt asked.

Pittman pointed at two of the SWAT guys, both young men. "Lewis and Darnell are going to head up Team B, which'll be in position on either side of the entrance to the trail. Here," he said, pointing with his pen. "We've got decent underbrush, bushes and whatnot on either side of the road. They'll be able to see any vehicles coming through, or anyone on foot for that matter. They'll let us know when the subjects pass, but they'll wait on our signal to start moving into position."

He pointed at two of the other SWAT guys at the table.

"Parker and Woodall will be with us on the closed trail. They'll belly-crawl it from the trail to the ranger station. Once Team B is in place, Parker and Woodall fire 38mm long range tear gas rounds through both windows. That allows the rest of us to move in from the trail on this side, while Team B moves in on theirs."

"Okay. What time is sunset tonight, anybody know?"

"Twenty-forty hours," Darnell piped up.

"Alright, it's almost three. Let's meet back here at six with the whole team. That work for you, Captain?"

"It works."

"Okay, guys." Wayne pinched at the bridge of his nose. "Let's not do anything the Hardy Boys wouldn't do."

⚓ ⚓ ⚓

At 11:02 that night, Maggie knelt at the base of a scrub pine on the closed ATV trail. Mosquitos squealed in her ears like radio-controlled helicopters and she'd given up on trying to wipe them from her neck. She wore a black Sheriff's Office windbreaker, and beneath that a department polo shirt, and beneath that her black body armor. The air was thick enough with moisture to make it hard to breathe. Her left ear itched continuously from the Earhugger ear piece attached to her shoulder mic.

She was almost certain she was going to lose her mind from the heat, the bugs, the itching, and the rivulets of sweat that ran down her spine. Adrenaline made it impossible to ignore anything.

She and four other deputies were squatting or kneeling in a line behind Wyatt, James, the SWAT guys and Captain Pittman, who were squatting or kneeling in their own line. It was completely black outside, the moon overwhelmed by storm clouds that promised rain at any moment.

No one spoke. Sound carried in funny ways across this flat land and radio comm was limited to Captain Pittman, Wyatt, and the leader of the team across the field. At 10:55, he'd let them know that a car with three people inside had passed them, headed for the lookout. They could see the headlights as it pulled in. Five minutes earlier, they got word that a second car had passed, this one carrying two people.

They could hear car doors closing and the faint sound of boots on wood as the visitors made their way up the ramp to the lookout, then the creak of a seldom-used door.

Darnell and Parker had started on their crawl for the structure as soon as the door shut again.

Now they waited. Maggie could barely make out Wyatt and the other officers. They were just blotches of black ink on a black piece of paper. Sweat dripped into her eyes, and as she blinked the salt away, they heard the distinctive, hollow *pop pop,* almost imperceptible as two separate shots, as Darnell and Parker fired the tear gas rounds through the windows.

"SWAT, go!" Maggie heard Pittman snap in her earpiece, and Pittman and his men rushed the field. She pulled her .45 from her holster and got ready. Twenty seconds later came Wyatt's command and Maggie jumped up, her thigh muscles protesting, and she, Wyatt, and the rest of the deputies started running.

Maggie heard nothing but boots thudding the ground for a few seconds as they ran, then she heard the wooden door slam open, and a lot of feet on wood. A few seconds later she could hear the SWAT members up ahead yelling "Hands on your head!" and "Face down, face down!"

By the time she, Wyatt and her fellow deputies arrived at the lookout, the SWAT guys had five men on the ground. Near one of them was a backpack that had fallen open. Two stacks of bills had spilled onto the ground.

Within thirty seconds, the SWAT guys had disarmed and handcuffed all five men. Maggie holstered her weapon and wiped her eyes with the back of her hand as the men were jerked to their feet.

None of them was Richard Alessi.

⚓ ⚓ ⚓

Four hours later, Maggie sagged against the wall in the small room that was connected by a one-way glass window to one of their two interrogation rooms. James and one of his deputies were still interviewing the second of the two buyers out of Gainesville in Room 1. Wyatt had gotten fed up with Joey Truman, who "didn't know nothin'," especially when asked about Alessi.

Now he sat across from Gary Barone, who had been holding the only meth at the scene, barely more than three grams. They'd been in there for almost an hour, with little to show for it.

Maggie watched as Wyatt slapped a file shut and raised a hand to the deputy at the door.

Wyatt got up, stretched his legs, and walked out, as the deputy moved to escort Barone back to his cell. A moment later, Wyatt walked into the dark observation room and shut the door.

Maggie watched him as he rubbed his eyes and sighed. Then he slapped the file against his thigh for a moment as he stared at the floor. Finally, he looked up at Maggie.

"We got nothin'," he said. "We can charge Barone for possession with intent. It's not much, but it'll send him back inside for a year or so. Joey, he's dumber than hell, but even he knows he doesn't need to help us out on Alessi. We'll charge him with accessory to a bad guy and he'll be out on probation. The little creep has two priors as a juvenile and that's it."

Maggie nodded and folded her arms across her chest.

"No Alessi. No ten kilos," Wyatt said.

Maggie shook her head. "I don't know."

"Well, unless Alessi's cooking meth that can give you superpowers, I doubt these guys from Gainesville were there to pay $200,000 for three grams," Wyatt said.

"He was somewhere out there, with the rest of the stuff," Maggie said. "Barone and Joey give these guys a taste, and they call Alessi to tell him the money's there."

"Not a bad plan, really."

"Now he's in the wind and I don't know. I don't know about Grace."

Wyatt nodded and fidgeted with his mustache a minute.

"I think we should let Joey go," Maggie said.

Wyatt looked over at her.

"Pretty cold."

"Yeah. But she doesn't have a plan B. We're supposed to have him in custody," Maggie said. "Now he knows somebody talked to us and I can't call her. I can't go over there. I can't even warn her that he'll probably walk right back through the front door."

"He already did," Wyatt said. "An hour ago. It's been quiet since."

"We need to go over there."

"Not you. You don't, Maggie." Wyatt pointed at her. "You show up, and he just might put you and Grace and the Piggly-Wiggly together."

"Send James, then," she said.

"I am. We're letting him give this guy Rolfe another go first. Right now, Grace's best bet is if Ricky thinks maybe one of these buyers is his problem."

"Or we let Joey go."

Wyatt stared at the empty interview room a moment.

"I don't necessarily have a problem with that. But I don't know that Patrick Boudreaux will go for it."

"Patrick Boudreaux works as little as possible and he couldn't care less about some small time wing man," Maggie said. "That won't get his face in the paper."

"Well, lawyers are on the way for the out-of-towners and Barone. Truman's gonna be sitting here till a PD shows up in the morning, anyway. I'll talk to Boudreaux first thing in the morning."

⚓ ⚓ ⚓

Late in the afternoon, Maggie sat at the computer in her office, finishing up her report on Barone and Truman. Barone had been remanded without bail due to his parole violation. The Public Defender couldn't have cared less whether they released Joey and neither could Boudreaux, so the paperwork was underway.

Dwight, AKA Dudley Do-right, walked into the office, carrying a pink message slip in one hand and a gigantic Styrofoam cup of sweet tea in the other.

"Hey Maggie? Lafayette County called. They want some info on some guy you busted a few months back. Apparently, they're holding him on an assault with intent."

He handed her the pink slip and she looked at the message.

"Quinn Wilcox?" She tossed the slip on her desk. "Tell them to just take him outside and shoot him."

"Will do."

"Thanks. I'll call them back in a bit," she said, turning back to her computer.

"What time did you get out of here this morning?"

"I'm not sure. Shortly before I came back."

"You want me to go grab you a cup of coffee?"

"No, our coffee's crap," she said.

"Okee-doke."

Dwight started to turn away and Maggie sighed.

"Hey, Dudley? I'm sorry. I'm a jerk today."

"It's all good, Maggie," Dwight said, and shot her a grin.

"Hey."

Maggie looked up to see Wyatt leaning in her doorway.

"Come talk to me a minute," he said.

"See you later, Mags," Dwight said as Maggie followed Wyatt out.

⚓ ⚓ ⚓

Once they were inside his office, Wyatt shut the door. He walked over to his desk and sat on the edge of it and Maggie leaned up against the file cabinet by the door.

"What's up?" she asked.

"You heard from the girl?"

Maggie brushed some stray bangs out of her eyes and behind her ear. "No," she said.

Wyatt sighed and folded his arms across his chest. They stared at each other a moment, then Maggie got uncomfortable and focused on the palm tree outside his window. When Wyatt didn't say anything, she looked back at him.

"What?" she asked him.

"What are you thinking about that?"

Maggie shook her head and threw her hands up. "I'm thinking my hands are tied."

"It's troubling."

"Well, yeah," Maggie said with half a laugh that she didn't mean to be derisive. "I can't exactly swing by and check on her."

"James and Cooper went over there a little while ago and asked Alessi some questions," Wyatt said. "He didn't know thing one as far as his pals were concerned. Of course. They didn't see Grace, but they heard kids in the house."

"They didn't go in?"

"They asked. Alessi came out instead."

Maggie sighed.

"We don't have probable cause or a warrant."

Maggie chewed on a thumbnail and stared out the window.

"Maggie, there was no meth and no Alessi. Just a bunch of money and a bunch of pissed off bad guys. Any chance she was lying to you? That Alessi did this for some reason?"

Maggie shook her head. "No. She's scared. She just wants out. And Alessi doesn't dislike or have it in for anybody enough to let a couple hundred thousand dollars get impounded. It's not his style, anyway. He would just kill 'em."

Wyatt nodded and watched her for a minute.

"He had to have been waiting for a call or signal from Joey. He was probably waiting right down the road."

"You should go. What are your kids up to?"

Maggie looked at her watch. "Kyle's got a game at six."

"Why don't you go home, take a shower, and eat something?" Wyatt asked. "Go enjoy your own kids for the night, get your mind off someone else's."

"Yeah," Maggie agreed. "Are you leaving soon?"

"I have a meeting with the Mayor shortly, and then I'm supposed to have a conference call with Liberty and Bay Counties. By then, I'll be on my face, so I'm going to go home and sleep."

"Good," Maggie said.

They looked at each other for a minute, Wyatt with his long, muscular legs stretched out in front of him, and Maggie felt a pull to just cross the room and lean on him for a moment. She was a strong woman and proud of it, but not so proud that she pretended a man couldn't be a comfort and a relief. She wondered what it would feel like to just put her head on his chest and rest, and she realized that, in her imagination, it didn't feel as foreign as it should. She was almost positive that it would feel comfortable and right.

Just as she realized that they'd been staring at each other for a few beats too long, Wyatt spoke.

"I suspect that this is going to get difficult faster than I expected," he said.

"What is?"

"Staying professional."

"I'm sorry," she said, wondering if he was changing his mind, and realizing that this possibility scared her.

"Don't be," Wyatt said. "But, you're going to have to stop standing there looking at me like that."

Maggie felt suddenly and immensely self-conscious. "Like what?"

"Like I'm looking at you."

# ELEVEN

K yle's team was down 11-9 in the fourth and final inning, and it was their turn at bat.

Maggie was perched on a bench near the dugout, preferring to bypass conversation with other parents on the bleachers. Little Tommy Baines was at bat and Doug Raymond was on deck. Maggie watched Kyle put his batting helmet on in the dugout. He would follow Doug.

Kyle looked over at Maggie and she gave him a thumbs-up. He was one of the fastest runners on the team, but also one of the smallest, and one of the weakest batters. This was only his second year playing, and he had yet to master his batting stance.

Maggie was focused on Tommy in the batter's box and didn't notice Bennett Boudreaux until he sat down next to her.

"Hello, Maggie," he said.

"Mr. Boudreaux. How are you?"

"I'm good, thank you. You?"

Maggie nodded and looked back at the field as Tommy connected and made it to first.

"My grandson was supposed to have a game on the other field, but the other team had to forfeit," Boudreaux said.

"What team does your grandson play for?" Maggie asked to be polite.

"The Braves."

Maggie nodded again, then watched Kyle, now on deck outside the dugout and taking a few practice swings.

"Kyle, keep that back foot down, baby," she called.

Kyle turned and looked at her, gave her an "okay" sign and took another swing. His back heel still came up off the ground as he swung, costing him momentum and power.

"Hey, Kyle?" Boudreaux called, getting up. "Let me show you something, son."

Maggie watched as Boudreaux walked over to Kyle.

"Hey son, look here." Boudreaux took Kyle gently by the shoulders and turned him back around to face away from him. "Go ahead and get that bat up."

Kyle put his bat up over his shoulder and Boudreaux put his right hand on Kyle's right knee.

"Bend that knee, keep all your weight on this foot here," Boudreaux said. "And imagine that you've got a live scorpion under that heel. As long you stay on top of him, you're okay. But if you let him loose, he's gonna sting you. So if you lift that heel, you better already be running, right?"

Boudreaux looked up at Maggie and winked. She couldn't help the hair standing up just a bit on the back of her neck, and took a drink of her sweet tea as an excuse to look away.

Kyle thought a second, then nodded, as Doug struck out and headed back to the dugout.

"Alright, you go try that, son," Boudreaux said, and made his way back to Maggie's bench as Kyle headed for the batter's box.

Kyle's first swing was a strike, his second a foul ball. Both times, his back heel came up, though not as much as before.

"He's gonna sting you, son!" Boudreaux called. Kyle turned around to look at Boudreaux and Maggie, then nodded and got ready for the pitch.

Maggie and Boudreaux both stood up and clapped when Kyle hit a decent grounder out toward third base. The infielder missed it and it headed on out to left field. It was enough to get him to first, and Tommy to third. Maggie and Boudreaux sat back down as the next kid came to bat.

"Cute kid," Boudreaux said. "Looks just like his dad. Once he gets his batting down, he'll play like his dad, too."

Maggie looked over at Boudreaux.

"I've got sons your age, remember?" He said. "I've seen David play many times."

They looked back at the field, as the next batter hit one out to right field. Maggie and Boudreaux joined the cheering as Doug and Kyle both slid home and their teammate made it to second. Kyle looked over at Maggie, brushing the dust from his pants, his smile wide and proud.

"Good job, Kyle!" she called, and sat back down.

The next kid hit a home run, but the batter after him struck out. Kyle's team headed out to the infield. The score was now 12-11 in favor of Kyle's team. They just needed to hold the other team there. Maggie looked over at Boudreaux.

"Does my ex-husband work for you?"

Boudreaux squinted over at her.

"In what capacity?"

"In any capacity."

"No," he said. "He doesn't work for me. In any capacity."

Maggie nodded and turned back to the game. So did Boudreaux. After a moment, he spoke again.

"I enjoyed doing business with your husband when he was still oystering. He worked hard, and he worked hard because he wanted to do well for his family."

Maggie looked back at him. "Yes, he did."

"That new boat. He made a bad decision, but he made it for the right reasons," Boudreaux said. "There was no way for him to know BP was going to piss all over our bay."

"I know that," she said evenly. "I didn't divorce him because he went out of business."

Boudreaux nodded and held up a hand to acknowledge that.

"This other thing, well, again, maybe he made a bad decision, but he made it for honorable reasons."

Before she answered, Maggie looked toward the bleachers automatically, although she knew they couldn't be overheard.

"You think running drugs is honorable?" she asked him.

"I think wanting to feed your family is honorable," Boudreaux answered quietly.

"We were eating."

"On your paycheck," Boudreaux said. "That's hard for a man who values work."

Maggie shook her head. She doubted she'd ever spent ten minutes in Boudreaux's company before they found Gregory on the beach. Now he was giving her relationship advice.

"Maybe one day you'll be able to forgive him for his mistakes," Boudreaux said.

"You think I'm judgmental," Maggie said.

"No, I think you have standards that are difficult for anyone to live up to, including you."

They both looked out to the field automatically, as the parents on the other team applauded a base hit. Then Maggie looked back at Boudreaux and shook her head.

"What?" he asked.

"Until last Saturday, you only knew me to say 'hello' to. Now you're offering me advice on standards and ethics."

"Well, first of all, I know more about you than you probably think," Boudreaux said pleasantly. "Secondly, while I appreciate the irony of your being counseled by the town villain—"

"I didn't say that," Maggie interrupted.

"You don't have to. Look, it's all very polite, and usually more convenient, if we both pretend that you don't know I'm somewhat shady, but I think we can just be honest with each other."

"Okay," Maggie said. "You know, some people think maybe you're considering grooming me to replace Gordon Bellows."

"I thought you did," he said.

"You know what I mean."

"I said we could be honest, not stupid," he said with a smile. "But you're no Gordon Bellows."

"No."

"We'll go ahead and just admit that I have some business dealings that aren't as squeaky clean as others and that you know that. Everybody knows that," he continued. "So now we can just talk like people."

He spread his hands, waiting for some kind of agreement. Maggie just nodded.

"You have a very strict moral code. Everybody knows that, too, including me, and I happen to like it. I have one, too. It's different from yours in some ways, but I'd bet we'd agree quite a bit about what we believe is right or wrong."

"You think so, Mr. Boudreaux?"

"Yes, Maggie, I do," he said. "As we get to know each other a little better, you may find we're not as entirely different as you'd expect."

"How so?"

"Well, we don't really know that yet, do we?" Boudreaux answered. "But for starters, I'd say we both understand that law and justice aren't always the same thing."

Maggie felt those hairs again as they stared at each other. She still felt his eyes were a remarkable blue, but she was suddenly reminded why blue was considered a cool color. He was smiling, but his eyes were cold, if such a thing could be said.

"I work for the law," she said.

"But you *believe* in justice," he said. "So do I."

At that moment, Maggie had no doubt that Boudreaux knew what had happened with her and Gregory. She was also fairly certain that he suspected she'd made Gregory pay for it. What she didn't know was how he felt about that, or what he wanted from her.

"Within limits," she said quietly.

"But limits are such individual things, aren't they?" Boudreaux asked. "And so changeable. As I know very well."

Maggie wasn't sure how she wanted to respond to that, so she didn't. She heard a ruckus, on the field and in the bleachers, but she didn't look away from Boudreaux's gaze.

"Why are we having these conversations, Mr. Boudreaux?"

"Because I think, if things were different, if a lot of things were different, we would actually be friends."

Maggie looked at him for a moment. "I can't honestly say that's not true."

He smiled at her.

"As hard as you might find this to believe, I genuinely like you," he said. "And I'd like you to understand me just a little."

He looked over at the field. The teams were lined up and high-fiving each other. Kyle's team had won.

"Well, look at that," Boudreaux said to Maggie, as he stood. "The underdogs prevailed."

Maggie stood up as well.

"Why do you want me to understand you?"

He looked at her for a moment, his smile gone.

"Because one of these days, you'll probably need to."

They both looked as Kyle ran past them, smiling, on his way to the dugout for his things.

"I've got to go. Goodnight, Maggie."

"Goodnight, Mr. Boudreaux."

As she watched him walk away, she thought that maybe flies didn't fly into spider webs because the webs were invisible. Maybe they flew into the webs because the spider didn't really look so bad.

# TWELVE

told you to quit lyin' to me, you stupid little skank!"

Ricky had his hand wrapped so tightly around Grace's throat that it was hard to breathe, even through her mouth. The blood in her nose was running down her throat, and she didn't know if she was going to suffocate or drown.

She pulled at his large hand with both of hers, and she heard the pounding of blood in her ears over the sound of little Rose's crying. The baby was in her carrier on top of the kitchen table, just out of Grace's reach. Ricky had pushed the chair Grace was in almost to the wall when he'd grabbed her throat.

Ricky leaned over and stuck his face right up into hers. His pupils were huge, so huge that his eyes almost seemed black, and he was dripping now with the sweat, that telltale meth sweat that smelled of cat pee and rage.

"You want to keep lying to me, Grace? You wanna keep lyin'?"

She tried to speak, but there was no air. Her lips opened and closed, but nothing came out, or went in.

Suddenly he let go with a shove so hard that her chair almost tipped over backwards. She took in an involuntary gulp of air so big that it hurt her chest, and a sound came out of her that reminded her of when she was in labor with Rose. One hand went to her aching throat and she held the other up in the air. Ricky leaned over again, and put both hands on the arms of her chair.

"You got somethin' to say, now? You got somethin' true to say now, you ugly little tramp?"

"I didn't do nothin'!" she gasped. "I didn't!"

"How'd they know we was gonna be there, Grace? Huh? Explain it to me, then!"

"I don't know!" Her voice sounded like someone had made her swallow sandpaper.

He stuck a finger in her face.

"There was only a handful of people that knew we was gonna be there."

"I told you it wasn't me, Ricky!" She was starting to panic, to lose control of her fear, and wished she was able to take a deep breath.

Too fast for her to even try to block it, his palm came straight at her face. He grabbed her face in his hand and pushed. Her chair tilted backwards on its back two legs, and her head and the back of the chair hit the wall.

She flailed like a crab on its back, legs kicking, trying to find solid ground in the air or to right the chair so she wouldn't be hanging from the wall by her face. He pressed harder, and she was sure that if the walls had been more than cheap fiberboard, her skull would have collapsed on itself. She felt hot tears streaming down her face, and was surprised she had any left.

He leaned his weight into her through his hand and then pushed off. The suddenness of it, of being free, put her even more off balance, and the chair skidded out from under her. Her butt hit hard and she felt an electric shock in the base of her spine, but she scrambled to her feet as Ricky stepped closer to the table and reached out to little Rose's carrier.

"Baby's cryin'," he said, smiling as he grabbed the back of the carrier and gently rocked it.

Grace took a step and he pointed at her with his free hand.

"Uh-uh," he said, almost musically. "Don't you move."

Grace stopped, but it felt like her heart kept moving toward the table, like a bird fluttering to a branch, as she saw Ricky rock the carrier closer to the edge of the table. Poor Rose was just hiccupping now, gasping for air like her mama had done.

"You got something to say, Gracie?" Ricky said.

Grace tore her eyes from the carrier and looked him in the eye and the terror came up her throat and out of her mouth.

"I've had it!" she almost screamed. "I've had it with you blamin' this on me!"

He stopped rocking the carrier, just as it reached the edge of the table, but his smile was gone instantly.

"What'd you say?"

"You're so tweaked out you can't even think!" she yelled, one part of her mind wondering at the fact that pure animal fear sounded just like righteous anger. "What am I supposed to do if you're in jail? I don't have a job, I can't even get a job that'd pay for day care! How am I supposed to feed these kids if you're in prison? You think I'm stupid? You're stupid!"

For a moment, there was no sound in the room but that of the baby wheezing and coughing. Ricky went very still, and his eyes, boring into Grace's, were filled with violence.

Then his cell phone came to life in his shirt pocket. It was the Metallica ringtone that he used for Joey Truman.

Ricky pulled it out and stared at it a moment, then answered the call without speaking. After a moment, Grace could hear Joey speaking rapidly, his voice tinny through the phone.

"Where you at?" Ricky asked, looking confused. He listened as Joey spoke again, but Grace couldn't make out the words. "What do you mean they let you go?

Ricky listened for a minute as Joey talked, and then Grace heard Joey laughing. Ricky wasn't laughing.

"I'm not goin' to no bar. Just come over here," Ricky said. Grace heard Joey say something. "Walk. You got legs."

He disconnected the call and looked at Grace for a moment, then headed for the kitchen door behind her. As he came abreast of her, his hand shot out and he slapped the side of her head hard enough to make her neck hurt.

"Don't you ever call me stupid again," he said, and walked out to the living room.

⚓ ⚓ ⚓

Kyle was out of the Jeep first and ran toward the house, his baseball bag in hand. He patted Coco as she deteriorated at his feet, sidestepped Stoopid, who was running some kind of figure eight between him and the Jeep, and ran up the stairs.

Maggie reached back into the Jeep and grabbed the mail off the console, then slammed the door.

"Hey, baby," she said to Coco, and scratched her neck before heading for the house. "Shoo, Stoopid! Go to bed."

The rooster ran toward the chicken yard and Maggie walked up the stairs, Coco on her heels. Maggie flipped through the mail and stopped at the top step. Coco bumped into her, then went around her, as Maggie looked at the envelope.

There was no return address, just her name and address printed in the center. It had a local postmark. Maggie flipped it over, ripped it open with her thumb, and pulled out the single, folded sheet of paper.

It was just one paragraph, and looked like it was printed from a computer.

*Maggie,*

*I wanted to write you and tell you that I'm sorry for what happened back then. I was young and I was messed up. Maybe I'm still messed up. You won't have to see me around town anymore, but I wanted to tell you I was sorry before I go.*

*Gregory Boudreaux*

Maggie swallowed a sudden nausea as she stared at the letter. Then she flipped the envelope over again. It had been postmarked yesterday. She looked back at the letter, even though she wanted to throw it far away.

The letter was printed, not handwritten. It could have been written by Gregory Boudreaux, or it could have been written by someone else. But Gregory wasn't the one that mailed it. He'd been at his funeral.

Maggie looked toward the living room window as she heard Kyle moving around inside, and her hands shook as she stuffed the letter back into the envelope. She didn't want to take it inside, didn't want it tainting her home.

She dropped her purse on the deck and hurried back to the Jeep, opened the door and leaned in. She shoved the envelope inside the glove compartment. She had to slam it three times to make it shut. Then she locked the Jeep and made herself walk, not run, back up the stairs.

Less than five minutes later, she was standing in the shower, her face pointed into the spray.

She thought of Bennett Boudreaux. She knew he knew what Gregory had done. But somehow, she could see Boudreaux as a criminal, but she couldn't quite picture him being cruel. Then she thought about her dream the other night. She thought about someone else, there in the woods.

She turned around and grabbed the soap and her scrubby and began washing herself. She went over every inch of her body at least three times, even after the water had turned ice cold.

Layered somewhere above or beneath the scent of coconut and Kukui was the faint odor of molding leaves.

CHAPTER
# THIRTEEN

B ack in town, Bennett Boudreaux sat at his desk in his office at the Sea-Fair plant.

He preferred to work in the evenings these days; the place was quiet and he could think. The older he got, the fewer people he liked, and the less he liked even them. Working at night was also an excellent way to absent himself from his wife's incessant dinner or cocktail parties, all of which featured a lot of discussion on topics that held no interest for him. He could write a check to save the Web-footed, Ass-faced Crane without having to know what he was saving it from.

At a few minutes before seven, there was a knock on the metal back door, and Boudreaux went out to the hall and opened it. Sport stood there, looking agitated and nervous.

"Sport," Boudreaux said, stepping back.

Sport stepped in. "Mr. Boudreaux. Thank you for seeing me, sir."

"No trouble, son," Boudreaux said. He closed and locked the door, then held out a hand. "Let's walk back to my office, alright?"

He followed Sport down the short hallway and indicated he should sit in the old vinyl armchair in front of his desk. Boudreaux had a fancier office out front, but that was for impressing people he cared to impress.

Once Sport was seated and bouncing a foot on his knee, Boudreaux sat back down behind the metal desk, and leaned back in his chair.

"So, what's on your mind, Sport?"

"Well, it's about Gregory, sir."

"So you said."

Sport studied the pictures on the wall behind Boudreaux, then the paperweight on his desk, before finally looking back at him. "Are you real sure he killed himself?"

Boudreaux looked at him for a moment before answering. "That's what the medical examiner decided."

"What do you think?"

"Why?"

"Well, you know, like a week before he died, he called me up and said he was planning on leaving," Sport said. "He said he was thinking about Costa Rica or someplace like that."

"Gregory came and went on a regular basis, son. It didn't seem to do much good. Maybe he figured it wouldn't help this time, either. He wasn't doing very well lately, even for him."

"Maybe." Sport watched his bouncing foot like someone else was bouncing it.

"Spit it out, Sport," Boudreaux said quietly.

"Well, sir. It's—that cop, the one that investigated the case. I saw it in the paper."

"Maggie Redmond."

"Yeah." Sport seemed to gather his wits about him, if that were possible. "The thing is, they had a history. Long time ago."

He waited for Boudreaux to ask, but Boudreaux didn't.

"He raped her."

Boudreaux scratched at his left eyebrow with one finger. "I know that."

"You know? How?"

"He told me. The night before he shot himself."

Sport seemed to be trying to reorganize his thoughts. Boudreaux wished him Godspeed.

"My question, Sport, is how do you know?"

Sport swallowed and worked hard at looking Boudreaux in the eye. "Well...I was there."

Boudreaux hadn't expected that at all. He took a slow breath and let it out just as slowly, never taking his eyes from Sport's. "I see." He took his time choosing his words. "And did you take part?"

"No! No, I didn't want anything to do with it."

"But you didn't try to stop it, either."

"Well, no. I don't even think she knew I was there." He waited for Boudreaux to respond, but Boudreaux just watched him calmly. "We were high, you know? It was fall break of our freshman year at Tulane, we were all jacked up on coke. I don't do that anymore, but we...you know, we got high then."

Boudreaux knew Sport wanted him to say something, but he didn't care to make it that easy.

Finally, Sport broke the silence himself. "And now, she's the one that investigated his death?"

Boudreaux continued to stare at the fool for a moment before he finally spoke. "I see what you're getting at, Sport. But it's not that easy to fake a suicide by gunshot, you know."

"I bet it's a lot easier if you're a cop. And why would she stay quiet all these years, especially after she became a cop, unless she wanted to get revenge herself or something?"

"You say that because you're not a woman."

"How do you mean?"

"If you were violated by a hopped-up college kid, you probably wouldn't talk about it much, either."

Sport swallowed again. "Well, I'm just saying, I think it looks funny. Her being on the case and everything. I mean, haven't you even considered it, since, you know...you know?"

"I consider everything," Boudreaux said. "And I'm taking care of Maggie Redmond."

"I mean, I'm glad she never said anything, obviously. I mean, not just for Gregory, but it would have looked really bad for you, too. It would look bad now." Sport picked nervously at a thumbnail. "For the family's reputation."

Boudreaux put his elbows on his desk and put his chin on his folded hands. "You've spent a great deal of time in my home over the years, Sport. You're practically family. You know as well as anyone that family comes first for me, at all cost."

"That's true, sir. I know that to be true."

"You also know that I like to cut to any chase that might be involved in a given conversation, so I'd like you to go on and get to the rest of your reason for being here."

Sport's foot stopped bouncing. Boudreaux was pretty sure it was an act of extraordinary will.

"Well, sir, you know, I'd been talking to Gregory about going in with me on this new venture I've had in mind, a pop-up gourmet deal back in Atlanta," Sport said. "I think it has real potential. But without Gregory's help with start-up, well, I'm kind of at loose ends. And to be honest, I'm flat broke."

"I see." Boudreaux put his hands on his desk. "So, you're hoping that I might help you out financially."

"Well, funding. I thought you might see that it could be a good investment. I wouldn't straight up ask you to just hand me some money. That would seem too much like I was asking you to pay me for something and that's not what I mean to say at all. I'm not stupid."

"No, son. You're not stupid." What Boudreaux meant was that Sport would actually have to apply himself to achieve stupidity, but he saw no point in being clear.

"Thank you, sir."

Boudreaux couldn't help smiling. "Here's the thing, Sport. You know me well enough to know that I don't hand anybody anything. Even if I did, that would make all this seem uncomfortably like something that you just said it isn't, am I right?"

Sport seemed to let that ping around in his head for a second before he understood it. "Well, sure."

"At the same time, my first priority is to do what I need to do for the good of the family. For all of us."

"Yes, sir."

"Additionally, Gregory's ill-timed passing has left me with a vacancy here at the plant."

"Sir?"

Boudreaux stood up slowly and came around the desk. "Come take a walk with me, Sport."

Sport stood up uncertainly, then followed Boudreaux out of the office.

"You see, we're just about done with our expansion here at Sea-Fair," Boudreaux said as he led Sport down the hall. "Gregory was going to move over here from the other office and oversee our new fish division. Oysters and shrimp just aren't cutting it these days, as you probably know."

"Sure," Sport said.

Boudreaux opened a steel door and flipped on a wall switch. "We're not operational yet, we've got an electrical inspection coming up next week and we haven't hired a crew yet, but I'm pretty proud of what we've done here."

The room was huge and everything in it brand new. It smelled of paint and sheetrock and sawdust. There were a dozen stainless steel tables in three rows of four, each with built-in drawers and overhead lights that were just now blinking to life.

Thick, industrial hoses with sprayer nozzles hung from the ceiling over each table, and there were floor drains spaced evenly around the room in the concrete floor.

Boudreaux swept a hand toward one wall. "Over here, we have three top of the line walk in freezers." He pointed his hand to the far wall, where a set of wooden steps led up to an office with plate glass windows. "Up there is what would have been Gregory's office."

"I don't understand, Mr. Boudreaux."

"Well, son. You, too, have an opportunity to be overpaid, underworked, and largely ignored. All you have to do is make sure people work, that they get paid, and that nobody slices off a thumb while they're fileting a grouper. This also makes our arrangement a little more palatable for me and profitable for you."

"You're offering me a job?"

"That's correct."

Sport took a few steps past Boudreaux and looked around. "But I don't really know anything about fish."

"Neither did Gregory." Boudreaux came up behind Sport and slapped a hand down on his shoulder. "I think this is the perfect place for you."

⚓    ⚓    ⚓

Maggie went into work an hour early the next morning. This wasn't unusual for her, so no one questioned it, but at that early an hour, she was able to work in their small, on-site lab without interference.

Three of the prints on the letter were smudged by something that didn't leave fingerprints of its own, and she knew those smudges could likely have been made by someone wearing gloves.

She got a total of six full and clear prints from the letter and several more from the envelope. Once they were transferred and scanned, she took the sheets back to her desk, fired up her computer and signed on to the fingerprint database.

It only took a few minutes to determine that the prints on the envelope belonged to three different postal workers and herself. None were unaccounted for and none belonged to Gregory Boudreaux, but she was unsurprised.

The letter itself contained her prints and Gregory's. No one else's.

She stared at the prints on the screen, prints Wyatt had taken from Gregory's fingers to compare with those on the gun, and then she stared down at the letter and the fingerprints she'd taken from it.

She felt like snakes were crawling through her intestines. The idea that Gregory had even thought of her made her sick.

"Gee, you're early."

Maggie felt her skin try to leave her bones, and she looked up to see Wyatt standing in the doorway. She slid the fingerprint sheet and letter under some other papers on her desk as he made his way over to her, two cups from Café Con Leche in his hands. It was too late to clear her screen without being obvious, so she hit Print.

Wyatt stopped beside her chair and looked at the screen as the printer whirred across the room.

"I figured you'd be done with your first cup by the time you got here, so I was extremely chivalrous and brought you one."

Maggie turned her chair around to face him and smiled, took the cup from him.

"Actually, I didn't stop this morning, so thanks."

She took a swallow as she felt him looking at the computer screen.

"Whatcha doing?"

"Oh, I'm trying to clean up a bunch of little stuff. I forgot to print Boudreaux's fingerprint report for his file."

"I did it, remember?"

"Oh. Okay, well, never mind."

Wyatt leaned up against her desk and she tried not to look away from him as he studied her face.

"You okay?" he asked.

"Yeah. Just tired. I didn't sleep too well last night."

Wyatt nodded. "She'll be alright."

Maggie scratched at her cup with her thumbnail. "Yeah."

She got up and stepped back just a bit so that she wouldn't be on top of Wyatt, then she stretched her back.

"Are you going to the Cajun festival tonight?" Wyatt asked.

"Yeah, I love it," she said. "And I could use a little mental break."

"I was hoping to go, but now I have to go over to Gainesville this afternoon. I'm just going to stay there tonight and come back first thing."

Maggie looked at him. He was almost eye-to-eye with her, which didn't happen often, and he was so close.

"That's too bad."

"Yes, it is."

"We could have pretended we were going to have a dance."

Wyatt looked out toward the hall, which was empty, then spoke more quietly.

"Yeah, and I could have contented myself with watching you."

"I usually just dance with my Dad," she said, shrugging almost shyly.

"I've seen you. That's okay, I would have enjoyed watching him, too. He's actually kinda hot once he gets going."

Maggie almost smiled.

"I'll have to tell him you said so."

"That oughta solidify our relationship."

For the first time, Maggie wondered what it would be like if she didn't work for the Sheriff's Office, if she could have just asked Wyatt for a dance.

Just then, Dwight stuck his head in the doorway.

"Mornin', Maggie. Hey Sheriff? You got a call on line two."

Wyatt pushed away from Maggie's desk.

"Thanks, Dudley."

"Sure thing," Dwight answered. "I'm outa here. Hey, Maggie. You going to the Zydeco Festival?"

"Yeah," she answered.

"Save me a dance, huh?"

"Always."

Dwight disappeared down the hall and Wyatt stopped in Maggie's doorway and turned around.

"Always," he said, mocking her. "See, I just need to get demoted and married, and then I can dance with you, too."

"Maybe next year," she said, smiling.

"I'd count on it," he said. "I'm going to go do Sheriff-y things."

He winked at her and walked off to his office. Maggie watched him go, then felt the smile fade from her face. She looked down at the papers on her desk and wished that what was under them wasn't there. Then she glanced at the cell phone on her desk and wished it would ring.

It seemed to be her day for wishing.

⚓  ⚓  ⚓

The Cajun Zydeco Crawfish Festival was an annual event sponsored by Bennett Boudreaux. It was held every year at this time to
celebrate the end of crawfish season in Louisiana, and Boudreaux
brought crawfish in by the refrigerated truckload from his business in Houma.

The event was held at Battery Park, just like the Florida Seafood Festival, which was a much bigger event held the first weekend in November. The Florida Seafood Festival was the biggest
seafood festival in Florida, and drew tens of thousands of people
for the weekend. Boudreaux's festival only served about a thousand locals and folks from nearby towns, but it had always been
a favorite of Maggie and her family.

There were Zydeco bands playing on the band shell all evening, and food trucks served up étouffée, gumbo, red beans and
rice, boudin, and beer. Vendors in booths sold T-shirts, signs with
cute Cajun sayings, and Mardi Gras beads.

Maggie and the kids found her parents by the boudin truck
and they all tucked into paper-wrapped, blonde sausages load-
ed with pork and rice and seasonings. It was just after seven, and
the event had been in full swing since five. The place was packed,
particularly the dance floor area in front of the stage.

Maggie tapped her foot and willed the music, the colored
lights, and the company of her neighbors and lifelong friends to
push all other thoughts out of her mind. She'd thought all day
about Gregory's letter, who might have sent it, and why. She'd
waited all day for a call from Grace, and thought of all the possible reasons it didn't come.

David stopped by for just a while, helped the kids win some
carnival games, stood with Maggie and shared a beer while they
watched the band, and then he'd gone home to his houseboat just
a few hundred yards away at the Ten Hole marina. Sky had long

since taken off with her friends, and Kyle had gone home with his best friend for a sleepover.

By ten o'clock, Maggie had had two beers, twice as many as she could usually manage. She wasn't by any means buzzed, but she was starting to feel a little more relaxed. She even joined Daddy for the Cajun Two-Step and smiled as she remembered learning that very dance at this very festival, when she was around ten or eleven. She'd had the same dance partner, too.

After their dance, Gray went off to sit with Georgia at one of the picnic tables and Maggie grabbed a cold lemonade from one of the booths, and leaned on some crates by the stage to watch the dancing.

Bennett Boudreaux appeared alongside her with a plastic cup of beer in his hand. Maggie had seen him out on the dance floor several times, each time with a different woman, usually one several years his senior. His face was slightly flushed and his hair was damp at the ends, but he still looked pretty dapper in khakis and a blue striped shirt with the sleeves rolled up.

"Good evening, Maggie," he said.

"Mr. Boudreaux. How are you?"

"This is the best night of the year for me," he said, smiling broadly. "The one night that both of my homes come together. Are you enjoying yourself?"

"I am, thank you," she said. "I love the Cajun festival."

"Good, I'm glad to hear that. Did you get some crawfish before we sold out?"

"Oh, yeah, we got a bucket and polished it off."

"You here with your family?"

Maggie nodded. "The kids have left, but I'm here with my parents."

Boudreaux watched her for a minute and seemed about to say something, but then the band started playing *Dance de Mardi Gras*. Maggie broke into a genuine smile, and her foot started tapping.

"I love this song," she said.

"Well, let's go dance."

"Oh, no. I don't think—" But Boudreaux had already taken her lemonade out of her hand and set their two cups down on the crate.

"It's not right to just listen to your favorite song," he said, and grabbed her hand.

"Mr. Boudreaux, I appreciate it, but I really don't think this is that great an idea," she said as he led her out onto the floor.

"I've had worse," he said. "Can you manage the Cajun Jitterbug?"

"Well, yeah, actually."

Boudreaux turned and put a hand on her waist.

"Good."

Maggie was impressed with Boudreaux's dancing. He had a lot of grace and excellent rhythm, and once she caught on to his little improvisations and extra steps, she actually started to smile. It was hard not to; the man was having a great deal of fun and it had been a long time since she'd danced with anyone.

She was winded by the time the song was done, and ready to go back to her lemonade, and out of the eyesight of the people she was sure were finding this all very interesting. But a waltz came on and Boudreaux pulled back on her hand.

"Aw, come on, this is one of my favorites," he said, and put his hand back on her waist. They danced with their bodies at a respectable distance, but when she glanced across the dance floor, she caught the eye of Lily Boudreaux, who looked more pinch-faced than usual.

"I don't think your wife appreciates you dancing with me," she said.

"My wife doesn't appreciate me breathing," he said with a smile. "But she knows I love to dance. She, on the other hand, fears that dancing might scuff the soles of her $400 shoes."

"Well, she's looking at me like she thinks I have designs on you," Maggie said.

Boudreaux laughed quietly and winked at her. "Oh, if she only knew."

Maggie felt compelled to ask him what he meant by that, but the song ended and Boudreaux, thankfully, put a hand politely on the small of her back, and followed her off the dance floor.

When they got to where they'd left their drinks, Maggie's mother was leaning against the crate. She smiled at the two of them as they approached, but the smile was polite rather than genuine.

"Hello, Mrs. Redmond," Boudreaux said as they arrived.

"Hello, Mr. Boudreaux."

"Are you enjoying yourself?"

"Yes, thank you."

"Well, I appreciate the loan of your daughter," he said, picking up his beer. "You folks enjoy the rest of your evening."

He nodded to Maggie and walked away. Maggie could feel her mother's displeasure, and turned to look at her.

"Where's Daddy?" she asked, hoping to skirt what was on her mother's mind.

"He's shooting plastic ducks with Tom Garland."

Maggie smiled and took a sip of her lemonade.

"Maggie," Georgia said.

"It was just a dance, Mom."

"No, it was Maggie Redmond of the Sheriff's Office, dancing with Bennett Boudreaux."

Maggie sighed. "I know. But he made me smile and I dearly needed it. He actually has a certain charm."

"I wouldn't be half as worried if he didn't," Georgia said. "It's the charming ones that you have to be careful of."

"It's okay, Mom. He dances with the Mayor's wife, too."

"She's not my daughter. It doesn't look right." Georgia fiddled with the top button of her white eyelet blouse. "Maggie, you're not...you aren't attracted to him, are you?"

"Mom. He's sixty-something years old and he's married. To say nothing of the other thing."

Georgia frowned at her daughter a moment. "I just don't want you to get hurt, professionally or otherwise. And Wyatt."

Maggie put her hand on top of her mother's, which rested on the crate.

"Mom, it's okay, I promise. And right now, Wyatt is my only candidate for 'otherwise'."

# FOURTEEN

**M**aggie was at her desk late the next afternoon, when her cell phone vibrated and skipped around on her desk.

She turned away from the computer to look, and saw that the call was coming from Grace. She snatched up her phone and answered.

"Hello?" she asked, cautiously.

"Ms. Redmond?" Grace's voice was almost a whisper.

"Grace, are you okay?"

"I need to make this really fast. He's in the shower."

"Are you sure?"

"I haven't taken my eyes off the door."

"Are you alright?"

"Yes, but you have to come get this man."

"What's happening?"

"He saw y'all. I mean, he saw gunfire. He was in his car, getting ready to call Joey and see if the deal was on. Then he called and Joey didn't answer and he left with a quickness."

"Does he know you talked to us?"

"He thought so, but I don't think he's sure now."

Maggie heard Grace take a long, but shallow, breath. When she spoke again, her voice was softer, but she spoke more quickly.

"We got to get out of here. He says we're leaving. He's taking a shower, first time in days, then he says we're going to Jacksonville to sell some of this stuff."

Maggie jumped up, her chair rolling back to hit the wall as she strode out of the office. "The drugs are there?"

"They're in the car, under the back seat. There's a compartment under there."

Maggie opened Wyatt's door without knocking. Wyatt stood up behind his desk as she walked across the room.

"The Monte Carlo?" Maggie asked.

"No, his car. It's a black Toronado."

"Grace, I need to put you on speaker, okay? It's just me and Sheriff Hamilton."

"Um, okay."

Maggie put the phone on speaker and set it on Wyatt's desk. She pointed at the phone and mouthed, "Drugs are there." Then she leaned in closer to the phone.

"Did he say when he's leaving for Jacksonville?"

"He said he wanted to rest for like an hour after his shower, then we're leaving."

"And he said you're all going?"

"Yeah, only I'm pretty sure if me and the kids get in that car, nobody's ever gonna see us again. You gotta get him this time. You're just gonna have to get him."

Wyatt held up a finger and spoke. "Grace, did Joey Barone ever show up over there?"

"Yeah, night before last."

"Is he still there?"

"Yeah. He's in the trunk."

Wyatt picked up his desk phone and pushed an extension button.

Maggie got a sinking sensation in her stomach. "Can you get out? Grace, you and the kids need to get out of the house."

"I think so. When he's sleeping maybe. But there's nowhere to go out here, to hide."

Wyatt spoke quietly into the phone. "Pittman, I need you and some of your guys, right now. We've got a possible hostage situation. How fast can we scramble to Houser Road?"

"Grace? Hold on a second," Maggie said and looked at Wyatt.

"Alright, get over to my office and I'll brief you. We need to go in quiet." Wyatt hung up. "Twenty minutes."

"What'd he say?" Grace asked.

"Grace, we're going to be there in twenty minutes. We'll be there, somewhere. I need you to get you and the kids out if you can."

"I'll figure it out. There's a—" Grace was silent for a moment. "He just turned the water off. There's an old chicken house on the lot next door. If we're out, that's where we'll be."

"Grace, be—" Maggie stopped when she saw the call disconnect. She started to say something to Wyatt, but Pittman rushed in.

"I'm here. The guys are getting geared up. What do we have going on?" Pittman asked.

Wyatt reached into a closet and pulled out his black body armor vest.

"Same guy from the other night," Wyatt said, getting his vest on. "He's at his house on Houser Road. I'll get you the house number, but it's the only house on the block where it dead ends. Blue."

"I know it," Pittman said.

"I'm going," Maggie said to Wyatt.

Wyatt paused in securing the Velcro straps on his vest. He seemed about to say "no."

"Go get your gear on," he said instead.

Maggie shoved her cell phone into her back pocket, ran back to her office, and grabbed her vest off of the small coat rack behind the door. She put it on over her SO tee shirt, slapped the Velcro in place, and then walked around her desk.

She opened one of the bottom drawers and pulled out her ankle holster, with her department-issued Glock 23. She yanked up the right leg of her jeans and strapped it on. Then she grabbed her keys and hurried back to Wyatt's office.

"How many kids, Maggie?" Wyatt barked as soon as she walked through the door.

"Three. Two toddlers, boy and a girl, and an infant girl." Maggie felt hot tears trying to form in her eyes, and she looked down, pulled out her service weapon, and checked it unnecessarily.

⚓　⚓　⚓

Grace heard the sink faucet turn on as she scurried from the end of the hall, back into the kids' room. Jake and Tammi watched her from the rug, where they were rocking the baby in her carrier. She fumbled with the phone's power button, got it switched off, and shoved it into the open toy box under some stuffed animals.

She had just turned around and picked one of the kid's backpacks off the floor when Ricky stopped in the doorway, a towel around his waist.

"What are you doin'?" he asked her.

"I'm just gonna pack a couple things for the kids to do in the car," she said.

"They don't need much."

Since she'd hung up the phone, Grace's mind had been scrambling for a plan. What she'd decided was that she needed to get them into the kitchen. Ricky had made them stay in the kids' room almost all day, while he packed his things and made some calls in the living room.

"The kids are hungry," she said. "Can we stop somewhere on the way to Jacksonville?"

"No, we can't stop," he said, his lip curling up. "I got people waitin' on me. Go make 'em some Spaghetti-Os or something, 'cause I don't want to hear them whining in the car."

"Okay. Do you want me to fix you a sandwich, baby? You haven't eaten in days, Ricky."

"No. I gotta lay down for like an hour, 'cause we're drivin' straight through. Just hurry up and make sure those kids are quiet."

"Okay," Grace answered as he turned and walked toward their room. "I'll pack you some sandwiches, okay, baby?"

He didn't answer, just shut the door.

"C'mon, kids, come with Mama Grace," she said, picking up the carrier. "Let's go in the kitchen."

The kids followed her down the hall, past Ricky's bedroom door, walking carefully, even on the blue shag carpet. Grace led them into the kitchen, and put the carrier down on the kitchen table.

The table was rectangular and Grace had set it long ways under the kitchen window, with two chairs on one side and two on the other, so the kids could watch the squirrels in the back yard while they ate.

"Jake, you sit here, and Tammi sit down here," Grace almost whispered.

Then she leaned over and looked out of the open window, but she didn't see anything but the kids' outside toys, and the lawn chair she sat in with the baby when she watched the kids play or sprayed them with the hose. When he was gone, she was going to get chairs for the kids, too, little kid-sized lawn chairs, so they could eat outside when it was cool.

Grace hurried quietly over to the fridge and took out some string cheese and apple slices for the kids and set them on the table.

"Just a snack, okay? Mama Grace is gonna fix you something better later."

Tammi put her blue bear, Binky, in the seat next to her and started unwrapping her cheese. Grace looked toward the hallway and listened, but heard nothing. Then she leaned over, got her fingers around the edges of the warped screen and started wiggling it, careful not to make any noise.

"What you do, Mama Gray?" Jake whispered.

"Shh, Mama's busy. It's okay." Grace got the screen loose, and hung it flat out the window as far as she could reach. There was only one other window on this side of the house, maybe eight feet to the right, and that was Ricky's room. They couldn't go out one of the doors, because Ricky had locked the deadbolts and taken the keys. They needed to go this way, and she needed to do it right.

She squinted up her eyes as she let it the screen fall into the grass. It didn't make a sound.

She took a deep breath and let it out slowly. Then she stood and waited, watching out the window and gently rocking the carrier in the hope that Rose would stay asleep. She just needed to wait a few minutes, just long enough for either Ms. Redmond to come or for him to fall asleep. If the police weren't there in a few minutes, she was going.

⚓  ⚓  ⚓

Maggie, Wyatt, two deputies and two SUV-loads of SWAT parked their cars diagonally across the road at the corner, then bailed out. The house was just a few hundred yards down on the right. Between the house and the officers was one overgrown lot. There was a falling-down wooden shed at the back of the grown-up lot, and alongside it, dividing the lot from Alessi's property, was a wooden privacy fence that was warped and weathered and had huge gaps in it.

They all drew their weapons, and headed for the lot next to Alessi's. By arrangement, Wyatt and half the team went in the direction of the front of the house, the rest of the SWAT guys headed for the middle of the property, and Maggie and two SWAT guys toward the shed.

The two guys with Maggie were supposed to go through the back door. Maggie had been ordered by Wyatt to stay by the shed with Grace and the kids if they were there. If they weren't, they were to get Plan B from Pittman.

They weren't there. Maggie and the SWAT guys rounded the back side of the shed and found no one. From there, they had a clear view across the yard and back of the house. Two windows, one door, no kids.

Maggie swallowed hard as one of the guys depressed his mic button and whispered.

"This is Stephens. No one here."

Pittman's hushed voice came through Maggie's earpiece, too. "How's the back?"

"Nothing," Stephens answered.

"Get in position and await my order."

The two SWAT guys bent over and ran across the yard soundlessly, beneath the two windows and to the tiny back stoop. They positioned themselves on either side of the door.

Maggie was about to wipe the sweat from her forehead before it hit her eyes, when a child's legs appeared out the window, and then he was dropped the couple of feet down into the grass. It was the little boy.

The SWAT guys both looked, and Maggie stood a bit straighter, held up her hand. She depressed her mic button. "I've got a kid coming out one of the back windows," she said, her voice hushed.

"Copy. Await my order," Pittman said.

She stepped to the very edge of the shed and waved the boy over as he stared at her, confused. He ran toward her in his bare feet. She grabbed him as he reached her, and sat him down up against the back wall of the shed. When she looked back again, the little girl was already standing in the grass, holding her hands up toward the window.

The baby carrier was coming out. The little girl grabbed the handle with both hands and lowered it to the ground.

Maggie saw the two SWAT guys look at each other and then look back at the carrier. The closer one looked ready to move. The little girl was trying to carry the carrier without letting it drag on the ground.

Maggie held up her hand again, then bent over and started across the grass. As she crossed the side yard, she saw Wyatt and the other men running across the grass at their end of the house. The quick glimpse she got of Wyatt's face as he saw her told her that she was in trouble, but she had no time to think about it.

She had just reached the little girl when Grace's upper half appeared through the window. She looked like she was going to try to slide out. Maggie ran to her, put Grace's arms around her neck, and pulled her out, grateful that it was almost noiseless.

She shoved Grace toward the baby and the little girl and waited underneath the kitchen window while Grace ran with the carrier in one hand and the little girl's hand in her other.

They had just cleared the other window when the little girl twisted away and turned around. She ran a few steps toward Maggie.

"Binky!"

The world stopped for just a second. Maggie heard nothing but the blood pounding in her ears, then, from inside the house, very close, "Shut the hell up!"

The next ten seconds or so passed so slowly and yet they were so fast that Maggie was unaware of thought. There was only the adrenaline and the blood in her ears.

She ran toward the little girl, who had frozen in place, just ten feet away. As she took her first step, she heard the back door as the SWAT guys broke through it, and further away, she heard the front door breached.

Maggie saw Grace put the carrier down and start to run back toward Maggie and the girl. Maggie saw her mouth open wide, but she didn't hear her make a sound.

Just as she reached the little girl, Maggie heard a sound above or behind her. Maggie grabbed the girl's arm near the shoulder and slung the child toward Grace. She landed on her butt in front of Grace, and Maggie saw Grace bend over to pick her up.

Then Maggie heard glass shattering, and she turned around and started to raise her service weapon. Alessi was already in the air, his legs pumping

He came down on top of her, and they both went down, Maggie on her back and Alessi on his knees. Maggie felt one of Alessi's knees grind into her left thigh as they landed. His other knee made a sickening sound as it hit the ground. The earth seemed like it would punch right through Maggie's back and, as her arms hit the ground, her weapon flew out of her hand and skittered a few feet away.

Maggie vaguely heard thumping and yelling inside as Alessi leaned over her, his hip bone pushing the air out of her, and reached for her .45. Maggie pulled her right knee up and reached down.

It seemed like slow motion to Maggie, as Ricky straightened up and moved to pull the slide on her gun, looking down at her with hate and meth and fear on his face.

Maggie raised her right arm and shot him in the chest.

He bent backward, then fell forward on top of her, and his chest blocked all of the light from her vision. He smelled of copper and gunpowder, soap and cotton, cat pee and adrenalin.

She heard the echo of the shot in her ears, more than once. More muffled and further away, she heard Wyatt yelling the same word over and over, a word she'd never heard come out of his mouth. Then there was light and there was air, and the weight was gone as Wyatt pulled Ricky's body off of her and dumped him to the side.

She saw Wyatt's face as he bent over her. His voice sounded like it was underwater, but she heard him yell her name. She opened her mouth but all she could do was nod.

Then she heard another man, off to her left, say, "Miss! Miss, please move back."

Maggie rolled her head to the left and saw Grace standing there on the other side of Alessi in her pale yellow sundress and worn sneakers. She was staring calmly down at Richard.

One of the SWAT guys came up behind her and gently put a hand on her arm.

It was then that Maggie looked down and saw that Grace was standing with one foot on Richard's outstretched hand, and Maggie had her first noticeable thought in minutes.

*Good for you, baby.*

# FIFTEEN

**M**aggie pulled the tee shirt over her head, her back and shoulder muscles protesting as she did. She dropped it onto the floor by her shoes and socks. Her bra followed. Then she unhooked her belt and started to lower her jeans. As was standard procedure, Wyatt had taken both her back-up weapon and her service weapon at the scene. After making sure she was alive, he'd said very little to her. Pittman had taken her preliminary statement while the paramedics checked her out.

Maggie had watched her fellow officers work the scene, then watched as Larry arrived to announce Alessi, as Maggie overheard one SWAT member describe him, "pretty damn dead."

Just before she and Wyatt had climbed into their vehicles, Dwight drove off with Grace and the children in his. They were going to Motel 6 overnight until the house could be cleaned up.

Maggie bent her left leg to pull her foot out of her jeans and her thigh screamed at her. It was going to be badly bruised, but nothing was broken.

Maggie was about to drop her jeans when she felt the weight of her cell phone in her back pocket. She pulled it out and kicked the jeans aside.

David answered on the first ring.

"Hey," he said, sounding surprised.

"Hey," she said, and her voice sounded hollow in the tiled shower area of the department's small locker room. "I need you to go get the kids and take them home. They're at the ball field, watching Sky's new boy play."

"You want *me* to pick them up?" They had a rule, Maggie's rule, that David never went anywhere with the kids unless she was with them. Maggie didn't want any of his associates associating the kids with their dad.

"David, it's important."

"What's wrong, Maggie?"

"I can't talk about it right now, just please take them home and wait for me to get there?"

"Yeah. Of course. Are you okay?"

"Yes. But please don't let them watch the news or anything, okay?"

There was a pause for a moment.

"Okay," David said.

"I'll be there in just a little bit."

Maggie hung up before he could say anything else, then she walked to the closest shower and turned on the water, as hot as it would get.

⚓　⚓　⚓

Maggie came out of the locker room, carrying her clothes in a plastic bag and wearing the smallest set of sweats that Wyatt had been able to find.

He was leaning up against the wall by the door to ensure her privacy. He pushed off the wall as she came out. She glanced up at him, then looked away as they walked to her office.

Terry, the investigator who shared her office, was sitting at his desk. He looked up as Maggie and Wyatt walked in. His kind face, more youthful than his forty years, was creased with concern, and he ran a hand over his receding hairline.

"You alright, Maggie?"

"Yeah, I'm fine. Thanks, Terry."

Maggie walked to her desk and picked up her purse, tucked her phone into it, and pulled out her keys.

"Hey, why don't you let me or Wyatt run you home, huh?" Terry said. "One of us can bring your car to you tomorrow."

Maggie shook her head. "No. David's taking the kids home for me, but I need my Jeep."

"I'll follow her home," Wyatt said, his hands on his hips.

"You don't need to. I'm fine."

Wyatt was already turning to leave. "Let's go."

Maggie followed him out to the parking lot and couldn't think of anything to say before they parted to go to their separate vehicles. She climbed in, started the Jeep, and backed out. Wyatt waited, then pulled out behind her.

It was a twenty minute drive to get to her road from Eastpoint. The sun was just thinking about setting as they crossed the bridge over to Apalach, and Maggie felt vaguely sad that she was too numb to appreciate it.

Every now and then, she looked in her rear view mirror at Wyatt behind her.

They were on Bluff Road, less than a quarter mile from her dirt road, when her cell phone rang. She pulled it out of her purse and answered.

"Hello?"

"Pull over," Wyatt said.

She looked into the rear view, saw him on his phone.

"What?"

"Pull over up there on that turnaround." He hung up.

Maggie pulled into a small, circular gravel area underneath some trees. She watched Wyatt pull in behind her, and she shut off her engine when she saw him get out of his cruiser. She got out of the Jeep and waited.

He stopped a couple feet from her and took off his sunglasses. Maggie waited while he stared down at the ground for a second, then he looked at her and sighed. He stepped forward and wrapped his arms around her, gently but firmly.

She was startled at first, then she put her arms around his waist and held onto his back. After a moment, she put her head on his chest. He seemed angry with her, had seemed quietly angry for hours, but he felt like safety and strength and comfort.

They stood there for what seemed like several minutes. Then he got back in his car without a word, and she got into hers. He watched her pull out onto the road, then he turned and headed back to town.

⚓   ⚓   ⚓

When Maggie pulled up to the house, David was sitting near the top of the stairs, tuning his guitar, the one he'd given to Sky. He stood up, and Coco flew down the stairs, was overcome a few feet shy of Maggie, and collapsed into writhing. Maggie stepped over Stoopid, nearly tripping and/or kicking the rooster, and he let out one of his misshapen crows before running off to do something urgent.

Maggie knelt down and rubbed Coco, then looked up at David, standing there holding his guitar by the neck. She felt a twinge of déjà vu, like she'd left this morning and come back six years ago.

As she walked up the stairs, Sky opened the front door and she and Kyle looked out at her.

"Mom!" Kyle called.

"Is everything cool?" Sky asked.

Maggie made herself smile and raised a hand to them.

David stepped over to the door. "Hey, y'all, give your Mama and me a minute, okay? Sky, go stir that chili for me."

Sky looked at Maggie for a moment, then shut the door.

"Sky saw it on Facebook," David said.

"Ugh."

"One of her friends posted something," David said. "But they already knew you were okay."

He studied her face and Maggie finally looked away and perused the yard.

"You are okay, right?"

Maggie nodded and started to say something, but then she smelled blood and cat pee, saw the little girl running back toward her, and she turned around and sat down on the stairs. David sat down on the step behind her, set the guitar down, and wrapped his arms tightly around her shoulders.

Maggie's eyes heated up and filled with water. David kissed her hair, then rested his chin on top of her head. They sat like that for a few minutes, then Maggie sniffed.

"How long before dinner?" she asked.

"Ten, twenty minutes," he said.

"Can you play me something?"

"What do you want to hear?"

"I don't care. Anything."

David let go of her and reached for his guitar. He lifted it over her head and set it across her knee, picked a few strings, then started playing. He sang a Dirk Powell song she'd always liked, folksy and old and quiet.

Maggie leaned her head back on his chest and listened.

⚓ ⚓ ⚓

David stayed for dinner and they ate out on the deck.

Maggie allowed the kids to ask her some questions, but when they started sounding like they were talking about a TV show, David deftly changed the subject.

It was nothing like TV. Maggie never watched movies or TV shows about cops. They dealt so casually with human life and death, and even when the human dying was someone without redeeming value, it was never as incidental as entertainment made it seem.

In ten years on the job, Maggie had been fired on and fired her weapon many times, but she'd never come that close to dying, and she'd never killed anyone in the line of duty.

There was nothing particularly triumphant about it. There was just the impersonal finality of death and the cold, flat feeling that came from knowing she'd been very close to being the one doing the dying.

That night, after David had gone home, Maggie talked the kids into piling onto her bed to watch a comedy. After the kids had fallen asleep, she turned off the TV and the light, and laid between them, cramped but not wanting space.

She breathed in the scents of Sky's too-sweet body spray and Kyle's freshly shampooed hair, and let them push back the faint aromas of copper and burnt powder and cat pee.

# SIXTEEN

**F**or the next two days, Maggie shuffled her kids from ball games to pool parties and finally, to church summer camp for a week. She'd worked in her garden and around the yard. She'd had dinner with her parents to reassure them that she was, in fact, alive and intact, but she'd stayed to herself for the most part. She'd done what she could to not think too much.

Wyatt had called twice to check on her and fill her in on the news during the first two days of her required week's leave.

Maggie had shored up the fencing on the south side of the chicken yard, planted coral and lilac begonias in the boxes hanging from the deck, done seven loads of laundry, cuddled Coco within an inch of insanity, and cleaned out and scrubbed the fridge.

Now, late in the afternoon on Friday, she was headed into town to buy herself some of the foods that she loved and the kids couldn't stand. Overhead, clouds the color of newly-paved road filled the sky, and Maggie looked forward to curling up with a book and listening to the storm.

She had just stopped at the red light at 98 when her cell phone rang. Maggie looked at the number, then grabbed the phone.

"Grace?"

"Ms. Redmond, they're taking my children!" Grace sobbed. "They're just takin' 'em!"

"What? Who?" Maggie could hear one of the kids crying in the background, and people talking.

"Children's Services! They just came and said they're taking my kids!"

The light had turned green and a car behind Maggie inched forward. Maggie ignored it. "Are you back at the house?"

"Yes, we came back yesterday," Grace said. Then she yelled to someone else. "You just wait! I got the law on the phone! You don't go anywhere!"

"Grace, I'll be there in three minutes. You tell them I'm coming and they are not to take those children off the premises."

Maggie reached over and turned on her dash light, then gunned through the light and turned onto 98.

She got to Houser Street in fewer than three minutes. She pulled up to the edge of the yard, and parked behind an Apalach PD cruiser. Mike Waddell was standing by the open passenger door. In front of his car were a tan sedan with its passenger-side doors open, and a white SUV with a man waiting in the driver's seat.

Maggie grabbed her ID out of her purse before jumping out. "What's going on, Mike?" she asked, as she headed for the yard. He opened his hands and shook his head.

Maggie walked past the tan sedan. Baby Rose was in the back in a car seat, a young blonde woman in the seat beside her. Maggie walked past them and into the yard, and hurried toward the group of people collected there.

Grace was in her same yellow sundress and bare feet. She still had her phone in one hand, and she had the other arm wrapped around the shoulders of the little girl who was standing in front of her, hiccupping and gulping air.

A short, doughy woman stuffed into beige trousers and a silk blouse was holding a finger up at Grace and talking. Next to her stood a blond man in his fifties, who was holding a file folder in one hand and the little boy's hand in the other.

"Ms. Redmond!" Grace yelled as Maggie came to the group. "Tell them to get my baby out of that car!"

"Who are you, please?" the dumpy woman asked Maggie, looking disinterested in the answer.

Maggie pulled her ID and opened the leather case. "Lt. Redmond with the Sheriff's Office. What's going on?"

"We're removing the children from Miss Carpenter's custody." The woman said it as though Maggie ought to know already.

"Why? Do you even know this girl?"

"She was negligent in having them in this…environment, and in having them here in the middle of a violent arrest. This is not a safe situation for the children."

Maggie swept a hand toward Grace. "She risked her *life* to get these kids out of their situation!"

"She risked their lives by having them in it," the woman said, her voice raised.

"They were being held against her will!"

The woman took advantage of the fact that Grace reached up to wipe her face, and she pulled the little girl to her, handed her off to the blond man.

"No!" Grace yelled. "These are my children!"

"Mama!' the little boy cried.

"Mr. Howard," the woman said to the blond man, and he started walking the kids to the SUV.

"Please! You don't understand—"

"You don't understand, ma'am," the woman interrupted.

"Where are you taking the children?" Maggie asked her.

"They'll be placed in a caring foster home for the moment, and we're in contact with their father's parents. We'll be discussing possible placement with them after proper screening."

"Sure, 'cause they did a great job of raising *their* kid!" Maggie snapped.

"Miss Carpenter will be permitted to present her case," the woman said. "Everyone's just going to have to trust us and trust the process."

"Trust you?" Grace shrieked. "Three of my teachers called you people and you still left me with my daddy so he could keep putting his hands up my dress! You don't care! You take kids away from good parents and leave them with animals!"

The woman didn't deign to answer, simply started walking toward the tan sedan.

"No!" Grace yelled.

Maggie followed the woman.

"Hold up," she said, and the woman stopped, throwing a sigh in Maggie's direction.

"Can I take the kids? I'll take them," Maggie said it before she'd even thought it.

"No, you will not, and this is not the purview of the Sheriff's office."

"She loves her children!" Maggie said, forcing herself not to yell.

"Love isn't everything," the woman said, and Maggie wanted to punch her sanctimonious face. She held up a hand instead. "Wait here. Do not move."

She jogged over to Mike and spoke quietly. "This isn't right, Mike."

"I'm sorry, Maggie," he said, almost whispering. "They call and ask for an escort, we have to come."

"Who can we call?"

"I don't know. I mean, we're usually the ones that call *them*, you know? I don't know who you call *about* them. A judge maybe?"

Maggie rolled her eyes and thought a minute, but came up empty. When she turned around, the woman was getting into the front passenger side of the sedan and the blond man had started the engine.

Maggie jogged to the passenger window.

"What's your supervisor's name?"

"Nancy McFarland is our director. You're more than welcome to discuss this with her, but this isn't actually your problem."

Maggie felt dangerously close to pulling the woman out of the window by her face. "Yes, it is."

"Wait!" Grace shrieked, and Maggie turned around. Grace was running out the front door, a blue teddy bear clutched in her hand.

"Wait!" Grace yelled again, and ran to the back window of the car, which was closed. "Tammi needs him!' She put a palm on the window, but the blond woman didn't lower it.

"Give it to me, please," the other woman said, her hand out the window.

Grace put the bear in her hand and the woman tossed it onto the seat beside her. Grace leaned toward the window and looked in the back seat.

"Don't be scared! Don't be scared, Mama'll get you!"

The window hummed closed in Grace's face and the SUV and sedan pulled away. Maggie stood there with her hands on her hips for a moment, then looked at Grace, who was watching the kids ride away.

"I'll get someone to help us, Grace. I promise. They'll be back."

Grace turned to her, her pale, thin face wet with tears.

"They don't come back," she said. "When they leave them, they never come back to get 'em, and when they take 'em, they don't come back, either. I've known these people all my *life!*"

Grace's face crumpled and Maggie stepped to her and put her arms around her. Grace leaned against her, her face in Maggie's shoulder, and let out just one wail. Then she straightened up and wiped her face with the back of her hand.

"Grace? I'm going to find someone to help you. And I'll speak on your behalf. We'll go to court if we have to."

Grace nodded, but Maggie wasn't sure she was listening.

"You shouldn't stay here by yourself," Maggie said. "Do you want to come with me? Do you want to stay the night?"

Grace hugged her arms around herself and stood up a little straighter.

"No ma'am. No, thank you. I'm stayin' right here until you or somebody brings my kids back."

Maggie didn't know what else to say. She reached out and squeezed Grace's birdlike shoulder. "You call me if you need to. I'll call you as soon as I know something, okay?"

Grace nodded and Maggie hesitated a moment, then headed for her car.

"Sorry, Maggie," Mike said as she passed.

She nodded, then got into her Jeep and pulled away.

**M**aggie pulled into the Piggly Wiggly almost automatically, although she'd lost her appetite for spinach pizza and Ovaltine.

Once she parked, she grabbed her phone, slid through her contacts list, and dialed the State's Attorney's office.

"State's Attorney's Office," a woman answered.

"Is Patrick Boudreaux in, please?"

"I'm sorry, he's left for the day. Can anyone else help you?"

"No, thank you."

"Would you like to leave a message?"

"No. Thanks."

Maggie hung up and sighed. It was after five. The storm clouds were so low that she was pretty sure she could reach up and see how full they were. It was almost dark, though hours early for darkness.

She got out of the car and went in to find something that would make her feel like everything was as it should be.

Thirty minutes later, Maggie ran to the Jeep just as the first few huge drops began to fall. She tossed the bag onto the passenger seat and climbed in, and the sky fell the instant she closed her door. The rain sounded like hoof beats on her roof, and across the parking lot, the Sabal palms were thrashing.

Maggie pulled out onto the street and turned toward downtown and home. Hers was one of very few cars on the road. She wondered what the kids were doing at camp with this storm, and suddenly felt lonely.

She was at the one traffic light again, waiting to turn left, when she dialed Wyatt's number.

"Hi," he answered.

"Hey. How are you?"

"I'm fine. How are you?"

"Good," she lied.

"Are you currently engaged in a bullfight? Because maybe you shouldn't be on the phone."

"No, I'm driving. It's raining."

"Yes, I see that it is. Where are you going?"

"Well, I was sort of in the neighborhood, and I was wondering what you were doing."

"Oh. Well, I was watching a documentary on African seamstresses, but my dish crapped out. Now I'm standing on my front porch with an umbrella."

"What for?"

"I'm waiting for you."

"Oh. Okay," she said, and looked at the empty street behind her before cutting over to make a right instead of a left.

"Maybe you could hang up and drive with two hands so that we don't have to discuss your driving habits when you get here."

"Sure." Maggie hung up without saying goodbye and tossed the phone on the console. "Dink."

A few minutes later, she pulled into the driveway of Wyatt's sage green cottage, a block away from Lafayette Park and a couple of blocks away from the bay. She'd only been there once, to give Wyatt a ride to work when his car was in the shop.

As he'd said, Wyatt was standing on the porch when she pulled in, and he was halfway down the short driveway by the time she'd turned off the car. She got out to find him standing there in sweatpants and a gray tee shirt, holding a black umbrella over her head.

"Well. That's downright courtly," she said with half a smile.

"I have my smoother moments," he answered. "Come on in."

He led her into the house, and a small living room with wood floors and rattan furniture. It was cozier than she'd expected, though she hadn't actually expected anything.

"You want a towel for your hair?"

"No, that's okay," she said, ruffling her hair a little. "It's not that wet."

"Well, come on back here."

He leaned the umbrella against the wall and led her through the living room to a kitchen/dining room with French doors on the back wall. The rain was hitting the glass sideways and she couldn't see anything outside.

Wyatt walked around a tiled breakfast bar and into the kitchen area. "I was just going to have a glass of wine in lieu of cultural enlightenment. You want one?"

"Sure. Thank you." Maggie leaned against the bar as Wyatt grabbed another glass from an overhead cabinet and set it next to the glass and bottle of red already on the bar.

"Are you still mad at me?" she asked.

Wyatt poured them both some wine, handed her a glass, and took a swallow before answering. "I wasn't mad. Well, I was. But mostly I was scared. Men behave oddly when they're scared."

Maggie nodded and took a drink of her wine. It was sweet and full and warmed her throat and chest. When she looked up, Wyatt was standing there, looking expectant.

"They're taking Grace's kids away," she said.

"Who is? DCS?"

"Yes."

Wyatt huffed out a breath and took a drink of wine. "That sucks. But she can fight it, maybe."

"How much have you dealt with DCS?"

Wyatt looked at her for a moment. "A lot. Mainly with kids that should have been taken and weren't."

"I believe completely that the system needs to exist, but this one is broken. It's hard to fight a broken system."

Wyatt sighed and Maggie took a long swallow of her wine.

"I let her down," she said.

"How, exactly?"

That gave Maggie pause. "I'm not sure."

"A couple of days ago, you killed a guy, albeit a psychotic toad, and today the girl you were trying to help has lost her kids because she was with that psychotic toad. Hopefully, that's temporary, but either way, it's not your fault. You're just a little too damaged at the moment to see that yourself."

"I'm not damaged."

"Sure you are. You'd better be, otherwise you should consider changing your line of work. It's not like the movies. Having the power of life and death is one thing, having to use it is another thing altogether."

"Have you ever killed anyone in the line of duty?"

Wyatt leaned a hand on the counter.

"Yes. And I was drunk for a week, even though he was a child molester who had dumped a nine year-old girl out of a moving car the day before."

Maggie nodded and took a drink of her wine. For just a moment, it smelled of Cordite, and she heard Grace's words in her head. *You're just gonna have to get him this time.* She climbed onto the stool beside her, feeling a little weak in the knee.

"I could have shot him in the shoulder," she said.

"You think?"

Maggie looked at Wyatt and shrugged a little. "Maybe."

"I think he was a tweaker with a busted knee and a dead body in the trunk of his car. I think he was gonna blow your face right off your head and then let us shoot him."

They stared at each other a moment, then Maggie looked down into her wine, took another drink.

"Anything else you want to talk about?" Wyatt asked her finally.

Maggie looked up and took a long, quiet breath. "I'd like you to kiss me finally."

She saw one end of his mouth curl up just a hair before he made it stop. "Am I behind schedule?"

Maggie suddenly felt shy and didn't know what to say. Wyatt came halfway around the counter and stopped, leaned his elbows on the end of it. His face was inches from hers.

"Let me ask you a question, Maggie. Have you ever been with anyone other than David?"

Maggie swallowed, felt self-conscious about an unpopular answer.

"No."

"Have you ever kissed anyone other than David?"

"I kissed Will McKnight in eighth grade."

"Will McKnight from State Farm?"

"Yeah."

"He's gay."

"It was truth or dare."

"So, you've kissed a guy that you were in love with since, what, kindergarten—"

"Fifth grade."

"—whatever, and you've kissed a gay insurance agent."

"Well, he wasn't selling insurance back then."

"That's adorable. So, do you want me to kiss you to make sure it's okay to kiss someone other than David, or do you have some other reason?"

Maggie thought about her answer for a moment.

"I want you to kiss me because I think about it all the time, even when I'm not thinking about it."

"That's a really awesome answer," he said.

"Thank you," she almost whispered.

He straightened up and walked over to her and she tried not to swallow too hard when he put both of his hands in her hair. Even sitting on the bar stool, she had to look pretty far up to look him in the eye. It made her feel like a little kid, which was not altogether how she was trying to appear, so she stood up on the rungs of the stool.

"Well then," Wyatt said quietly, and then he kissed her.

It was not at all like kissing David, and once she got over the initial strangeness of Wyatt's mouth, and the initial strangeness of kissing the boss that she had worked and been friends with for six years, it was like nothing else at all.

And Wyatt was right; he was an impressive kisser. But when he finally pulled away from her a little, it was Wyatt's face that seemed just a bit flushed.

"Well," he said, with half a laugh. "I guess there's something to be said for practicing on the same guy your whole life."

Maggie smiled, somewhat relieved. All the same, she was finding it hard to breathe.

"So, are you still going to be thinking too much about kissing me?" he asked her.

This time, Maggie smiled wide. "I think I'm going to be thinking a lot, in general."

"Then we're in a heap of trouble."

Maggie stepped down off the stool, brushing against his solid chest as she got to the floor. He stepped back, but reached out and took her hand.

"Good trouble, though," she said. "Right?"

"The best kind," he answered.

"I'd better go. I have ice cream in the car."

"You should probably keep some ice cream in the car at all times. It gives us an out."

"Do you need one?"

"Hell, yes. Come on, I'll walk you out."

He held her hand as they walked to the door, then grabbed the umbrella and followed her out. The rain had let up a little, enough to see, but it looked like it was settling in for the night.

Wyatt let go of her hand when they got to the Jeep, then opened the door for her. He shut it once she got in, and she started the engine.

"Hey," Wyatt said through the glass, and Maggie rolled the window down. "Wait til you get a load of my slow dance."

He leaned in and gave her a gentle kiss, then stood up and raised a hand goodbye. "Be careful."

Maggie smiled and backed out of the driveway before she could say anything stupid.

# EIGHTEEN

Maggie finally got through to Patrick Boudreaux late Monday afternoon. It had taken four calls and three messages for him to call her back.

"What can I do for you, Maggie?" he asked.

"I have a problem with DCS. I was hoping you could help."

"For you?" he asked, and sounded surprised, but there was some happiness under there as well.

"No, for Grace Carpenter, the girl who gave us the information on Richard Alessi."

"The girlfriend."

Maggie wanted to say something snarky, but she needed Patrick's help.

"Yes. DCS took her children away Friday."

"I'm a prosecutor, not a social worker."

"You work for the state. They're state. I was hoping you might know someone who could help."

"No, I really don't," he said, and sounded less than upset about it.

"What about a friendly judge who might be able to help?"

"I don't work family court, Maggie."

"So you don't have any way to help this girl and her kids."

"Nothing I can think of, no. You can always vouch for her in court, if it gets that far."

"You really live up to your family's reputation, you know that?"

"Is that right? Well, our reputation doesn't seem to get in the way of you two-stepping with my father."

"It was a waltz, you putz."

Maggie disconnected and banged the cell phone down on the kitchen table. Patrick might work for the court and Boudreaux might be a crook, but he was three times the man his son would ever be.

She leaned on the counter and took a few deep breaths, willing herself to calm down. Then she picked up the phone again, looked through her call history, and clicked the number.

"Hello?"

"Mr. Boudreaux, it's Maggie Redmond."

"Hello, Maggie."

"I need your help."

"What is it?" Boudreaux actually sounded interested, which was more than Patrick had done.

"I've been working with a girl, a girl who got mixed up with Richard Alessi."

"Richard Alessi's a scumbag. But I hear he's a deceased scumbag."

"Yes. But now DCS has taken her children away from her. She's a good girl. It took a lot of courage for her to come to me."

"I'd say it did."

"She loves her kids."

"No offense meant, but I don't know anyone at DCS. Why are you calling me?"

"Because your son is useless."

Maggie hadn't meant to say that, but Boudreaux laughed quietly.

"I'm sorry, Mr. Boudreaux. I'm just upset. This girl deserves to keep her kids."

"Well, I know some people who might be able to weigh in her favor," Boudreaux said. "I can't promise anything, but give me a couple days to try and call in one or two favors."

"Thank you."

"You're welcome."

Maggie paused for a moment.

"Am I going to owe you something for this?"

"Yes, a drink. I'll call you," he said and hung up.

Maggie stood there for a second, realizing with some surprise that her hands were shaking just a little. She opened her contacts and called Grace's phone.

"Hello?" Grace's voice was expectant and hopeful.

"Grace, it's Maggie Redmond."

"I know."

"Listen, I struck out with the State's Attorney's office. It was kind of a long shot, anyway. But I have someone else looking into your kids."

"Are they a lawyer?"

"No, just a...just a friend, but he knows a lot of important people."

"Oh. Okay." Grace sounded deflated.

"It's going to be okay," Maggie said. "Don't lose your faith. Do you want to come here? Or maybe go get some lunch? Are you eating?"

"No, I'm fine. I'm staying right here until my kids come home."

"Okay, Grace. But call me if you change your mind. Or if you need something. Okay?"

"Okay. I will."

Maggie hung up and let out a deep breath. Then she went outside to look for something she *could* fix.

⚓    ⚓    ⚓

Maggie spent the rest of the day occupying her mind, mainly with Wyatt Hamilton. She was at loose ends, and needed to go to work or have her kids home. She'd be able to return to work Wednesday and the kids would be back Thursday night. She focused on staying busy until then.

She accomplished that by mowing the little grass she had in the yard, rescuing Stoopid from an old doghouse that no longer fit Coco, scrubbing the floors and thinking about Wyatt. Mainly, she thought about Wyatt.

When she went to bed, at the early hour of nine because she was so bored, she was still thinking about the way Wyatt smelled, and the way his mouth had felt on hers.

That night was the first one in recent days that was not disturbed by nightmares.

# CHAPTER
# NINETEEN

Wayne Stinnett checked his line, then padded barefoot across the deck of his Chris Craft to grab the Thermos of coffee his wife had made him. He opened it, poured a fresh cupful into his chipped Key West mug, and took an appreciative swallow.

He was an oysterman by trade, but had cut back to working the oyster beds just three days a week. Even so, most of his days off were spent on the bay, and sunrise was his favorite time to come out here to this area. The sea trout had a hankering to congregate near the causeway over to St. George early in the morning, and he had a hankering for sea trout.

He took off his Papa Joe's cap, and wiped at his mostly bald head with a forearm. It wasn't even seven yet, and it was already hot. His white beard itched from the humidity that promised the kind of day that would keep most people inside.

Wayne finished his coffee in one big gulp and set his mug down as he saw his rod bend toward the sea. He rushed over, pulled it out from where he'd jammed it behind the bench seat, felt the line, and started reeling. He could see it was a redfish, not a trout, but that was okay. Martha loved redfish, and he loved Martha.

As he parried with his fish, he looked up toward the causeway. He was at the high point in the bridge, where it humped up all of a sudden. It was a good seventy feet at this point, or so he recalled. His boat was a good thirty yards outside the shade line, but something made him look up at the bridge and he saw her.

There was a woman or a girl standing there, and at first he thought she'd pulled over to throw up over the side. But then she slowly climbed up on the wall and stood there for just a second or two.

Wayne had thought he was about to shout up to her, although he didn't know what. But, when he opened his mouth, nothing came out. And then she just bent over and fell.

Wayne knew they were too far away from each other for it to be true, but just before she started falling, with her little yellow dress whipping around her legs, he could have sworn they'd looked each other in the eye.

⚓　⚓　⚓

Maggie was half-awake and thinking about going back to sleep when her cell phone rang.

"Hello?"

"Hey, Maggie? It's uh, it's Dwight."

"Hey. What's up?"

"Well, uh, you know Wayne Stinnett?"

Maggie sat up. "Yeah, he's good friends with my Dad. Is he okay?"

"Well, the thing is, uh…he just called in a few minutes ago, after he called the Coast Guard."

Maggie jumped out of the bed, her heart pounding. "Dwight. Is it my Dad?"

"Oh no, oh, I'm sorry, Maggie, no," Dwight hurried. "But a woman jumped off the 300, out there at the hump. And, the thing is, there's a blue Monte Carlo up there and I ran the plates—"

"I have to go, Dwight," Maggie said.

"Wyatt's already on his—"

Maggie tossed the phone down and felt her chest cave in. Then she pulled on her jeans from the day before.

⚓ ⚓ ⚓

It took Maggie less than fifteen minutes to find the spare keys to her Dad's little speedboat and get to Scipio Creek Marina. It took another fifteen for her to get out to where a Coast Guard cutter, the department boat, and several fishing or oyster boats were congregated.

Maggie cut the engine and coasted up along Wayne Stinnett's port side. He was leaning against his starboard rail, watching the activity near the cutter.

"Wayne! Can you tie me off?"

Wayne turned and hurried over to grab her bow line, and tied her off as she hurriedly dumped two bumpers over the side between their boats. Then she grabbed Wayne's hand, walked up his hull, and climbed over the rail.

"Aw, Maggie. Dammit."

He rushed back over to the starboard rail and Maggie followed him. Ten feet away, Wyatt stood on the deck of the department boat with a couple of deputies, hands on his hips and cap in his hand.

"Wyatt?" Maggie called.

He turned, pulled his eyebrows together, and took a few steps toward her. "What are you doing here, dammit?"

"Dwight called me. Why didn't *you* call me?"

Wyatt took a few steps closer, leaned on the rail. "Because knowing is bad enough; you don't need to see it."

"We got her!" a man shouted from the Coast Guard cutter, and Wayne ran over to the other rail.

Two men reached over the side of the cutter, and two men in scuba gear were lifting something up. Maggie held her breath and watched.

First she saw pale, thin arms, and then birdlike shoulders and almost brown hair. When the men gently lowered her to the deck, Maggie noticed that there was a clump of seaweed stuck in her long hair.

She had forgotten Wayne was beside her until he spoke, his voice hushed.

"Why, that's just a little girl."

Maggie turned her back on the cutter and leaned back against the rail. She blinked a few times as she stared at the deck, then looked over at Wayne. He had taken off his cap and was blinking rapidly, but his eyes were filling anyway.

"Maggie, what could be so bad? Everything gets better eventually," he said, and his voice broke as tears slipped down his face.

*Not everything*, Maggie thought.

Wayne had served in the Marines with her Daddy, and was one of the funniest and toughest men she'd ever known. She'd never seen him cry unless he was laughing. She reached over and they hugged, then they both pulled away. Then she untied her line and jumped over the rail onto the deck of the speedboat.

Wyatt turned as she started the engine, and walked over to the rail of the department boat as she yanked up the bumpers.

"Maggie!" Wyatt called.

Maggie shook her head, eased off away from Wayne's boat and coasted past the cutter. The Coast Guard had laid Grace on a stretcher. Maggie looked at her as she slowly went past.

*Grace. You said you'd stay right there.*

⚓ ⚓ ⚓

Maggie stayed out on her Dad's boat for the rest of the day, cruising around the bay and sitting for a while, then finally dropping anchor near Little Towhead Island. She spent a couple of hours there, ignoring people who waved as they passed by on their boats, and drinking warm Dr. Peppers that someone had left in the cooler a long time ago.

Just before sunset, she pulled anchor and docked the boat back in Daddy's slip at Scipio Creek. She got in the Jeep and pulled out onto the street, intending to go home, but the aloneness of that struck her and she went one block and pulled into Up the Creek Raw Bar instead.

She was sitting on the back deck, nursing the beer she'd ordered an hour earlier, when Bennett Boudreaux spoke up beside her.

"Hello, Maggie," he said cheerfully.

Maggie looked up at him, and she must have looked a sight, with salty, windblown hair, a decent sunburn, and reddened eyes. His smile disappeared.

"Hello, Mr. Boudreaux."

"Are you alright?"

She half-smiled at him. "I will be eventually."

"May I sit?"

She nodded, and he sat down beside her, a glass of scotch in his hand.

"It's none of my business, but can I ask what's wrong?"

Maggie looked at him for a moment and swallowed. "The girl I was trying to help. She killed herself today."

Those brilliant blue eyes blinked a few times, and Maggie thought, inappropriately, how beautiful they really were.

"The girl on the bridge?" he asked quietly.

"Yes."

He crossed himself, then was quiet for a moment, and seemed to be searching her face. "Maggie, I'm genuinely sorry. I truly am."

She nodded at him. She believed him, too.

"I was still trying to find someone that might help. I'm sorry."

"Thank you, Mr. Boudreaux, I appreciate that."

They looked at each other for a good minute. Maggie saw concern on his face and she was almost certain that the concern was real. Finally, he slid his glass toward her on the wooden table. She picked it up and took a long swallow.

"Thank you," she said again, as she put the glass down. She looked away, not wanting to see someone who might or might not be her enemy looking at her with pity.

"Mr. Boudreaux, do you remember telling me that when you do something good in private it's because it's the right thing to do?"

"Yes."

"With all of your money and all of your connections, I bet you could do something for girls like Grace. For parents like Grace."

Boudreaux sat back in his chair and considered her, took a sip of his scotch. "Like what, exactly?"

Maggie huffed out a frustrated laugh. "If I knew that, I would have asked you to do it already."

"If the occasion weren't so sad, I'd be laughing. Not at you, at the irony of a cop trying to turn the town hood into a social activist."

Maggie had to smile at that.

"Do you think it's such a good thing to let yourself get so deeply hurt, personally, by your cases?"

Maggie thought about that a second. "Do you think it would be such a good thing if I didn't?"

He nodded at her, and they each took a sip of his drink.

"Are you here with your family?" she asked, to change the subject.

"No. No, a friend and I are headed out to do some night fishing," he said. "I just popped in for a quick drink while I wait for him."

Maggie nodded, then stood up. He stood as well.

"I need to get home, it's been a long day."

Boudreaux nodded, still frowning at her. "Are you okay to drive?"

"Yes," she said, and almost managed a polite smile. "That's all I've had."

"Well, then good. Go be with your family, Maggie."

She nodded again, then turned and headed for the stairs.

⚓ ⚓ ⚓

Maggie had intended to go straight home, but she headed east instead and pulled into Ten Hole down by Battery Park. She parked on the patch of grass that served as a parking area, and walked down the dock to David's houseboat.

He was sitting on the back sun deck, reading a paperback book. He looked up when he heard her footsteps and stood up quickly as she stopped by his gangway.

"Hey, baby," he said, and moved toward the gangway.

She held up her hand and he stopped.

"Don't get off the boat," she said.

"What's going on? You look awful."

"A girl jumped off the 300 today."

"I heard," he said quietly.

"I was trying to help her...but she just couldn't."

"Couldn't what?"

"Wait, I guess."

"I'm sorry, baby."

"She was Ricky Alessi's girlfriend. She was the one living with Alessi."

Some understanding passed over David's face, and he looked sad.

"I need you to understand. Her name was Grace Carpenter and she's dead because of the business that you're in."

"I don't have anything do with meth, Maggie, you know that!"

"It doesn't matter, David. It's all the same. It's all the same money and it's all the same people."

David blinked at her a few times, stung.

"She was three years older than our daughter, David, and she's dead because she was with someone who did the same thing you're doing."

They stared at each other a moment.

"I'm not trying to hurt you," Maggie said. "I just needed you to know."

Then she turned and walked back up the dock.

⚓  ⚓  ⚓

Bennett Boudreaux pulled back the throttle on his boat's engine and the noise level dropped as he slowed to a cruise. They were out past St. George, in the Gulf proper, one of Bennett's favorite areas to fish.

"I love night fishing," he said over the engine. "The quiet, the stars, the night sky. It's incredible. You really have to experience it to appreciate it, I guess."

He cut the engine and the boat slowly came to a stop. "This looks like a good spot."

He dropped the anchor and shook out his hands, tingling from the vibration of the wheel.

"It's important to take some time to enjoy the simple things. But like I said in the office the other day, family is my first priority."

He reached out and took Sport's hand.

"And you're just not family, old chum."

Then he threw Sport's arm into the dark, churning sea.

READ ON FOR A SNEAK PEEK

AT *RIPTIDE,* BOOK 2 IN

*THE FORGOTTEN COAST*

FLORIDA SUSPENSE SERIES

# AVAILABLE JUNE 2015

# AUTHOR'S NOTE

I truly enjoy getting to know my readers. We writers aren't as people-phobic as the stereotypes might lead you to believe. If you'd like to drop me a line, ask a question, or stay up to date on new releases and special pricing for my friends, please visit my website at www.dawnleemckenna.com

Also, you can read the rest of the Forgotten Coast series at www.amazon.com/Dawn-Lee-McKenna/e/B00RC14PPG

While you're there, I would be very grateful if you'd take just a moment to leave an honest review of this book.

# ACKNOWLEDGEMENTS

I am deeply indebted to several people for helping me make this series happen.

Thank you so much to the Betafish, for taking time out of their lives to read each chapter as it was written, and keep me from writing anything stupid or inauthentic.

I am incredibly grateful to John Solomon, executive director of the Apalachicola Chamber of Commerce, and formerly of the Franklin County Sheriff's Office, for helping me sound like I know something about law enforcement in Apalach.

To the real Wayne Stinnett, friend, mentor, and author of the bestselling Jesse McDermitt series, set in the Florida Keys, your belief in me has meant more than you know.

I could not have published this book without the help of three other fabulous professionals. Tammi Labrecque, of larksandka-tydids.com, your editing prowess was invaluable. Power to the Oxford comma. Shayne Rutherford, of darkmoongraphics.com, thank you for creating four beautiful book covers from thin air. Finally, Colleen Sheehan, of wdrbookdesign.com—once again, you have made plain words on a white background look like works of art. You amaze me, my friend.

# CHAPTER ONE

The sky over Apalachicola Bay, in the Florida panhandle, had just gone from orange to pink, and then blue. Here and there, small, wooden oyster skiffs dotted the shallow waters, punctuating the start of the long oystering day.

Further out, larger shrimp boats, their nets spreading like pterodactyl wings, were coming to the end of their day. One of those boats belonged to Axel Blackwell, whose twenty-seventh cigarette was dangling from his lips as he watched his crewmen, Daryl and Petey, swing the second shrimp net over to hover above the deck.

Axel was tired and irritated. They'd been out since seven the night before, trying to harvest enough shrimp to pay the two crewmen, pay Axel, and still have money to pay for the fuel they'd need tomorrow night.

Shrimping was all Axel did and all he'd ever wanted to do. His father had made his living with this same boat for forty-five years, and his father's father had died doing it, due to an unfortunate mixture of fuel leak and chain smoking.

Axel had come out to the bay straight from high school, and he was going to eke a living from it until either they drained the Gulf or the oil companies did it in for good.

He weighed the bulging net with his eyes as Daryl moved in to untie the rope at the bottom that held it shut. This was a good load. As long as there were some nice big ones in there among all the peewees, they'd do all right.

Daryl, big as a truck and blacker than good dirt, yanked the knot loose and stepped back as the load poured out in a rush, spreading out somewhat before piling up in a heap at the center. Petey, small, wiry, and gray in the beard, hopped over a writhing sea trout as it slid right at him.

They all stared at the three hundred or so pounds of sea life and seaweed.

"Oh, my sweet dear Jesus," Daryl said quietly.

Petey leaned over the side and threw up into the bay.

The tip of Axel's cigarette flared up as he inhaled, then he let a finger of smoke escape his clenched lips.

"Crap," he said. "We might want to get that crab off that foot there."

⚓ ⚓ ⚓

Maggie Redmond's long, dark hair whipped around her face as she ran the Sheriff department's speedboat at full throttle across the bay. She turned around and looked at Wyatt, her boss and the Sheriff of Franklin County, who was standing just behind her, holding onto the starboard rail.

"Hey!" she called. He looked over at her. "Steer for a second, would you?"

Wyatt stepped over and took the wheel, and Maggie dug a ponytail holder out of her jeans pocket and restrained her hair. She was short to begin with, but standing next to Wyatt, who was six-feet four, she always felt like she needed to stand up just a little straighter and display her holster a little more prominently.

Maggie took the wheel again, and Wyatt remained standing next to her.

"You know Axel Blackwell?" he yelled over the engine.

"Yeah, we went to high school together," she yelled back.

"Straight shooter?"

Maggie smiled, then couldn't help laughing just a bit. "Yeah, you could say that."

They were silent for a few minutes, as they passed St. George Island to the left, which sat five miles or so off the mainland. Hwy 300, or the causeway, or the bridge, depending on who was talking, connected St. George Island to the mainland like a suspended shoestring.

After a few minutes, Maggie pointed out to the west.

"There's the *Ocean Bounty*," she yelled.

It took them just a few more minutes to reach Axel's boat, which had dropped anchor before Axel called Maggie.

Daryl leaned over the port side as Maggie cut the engine and coasted over, then he grabbed the line Wyatt tossed at him. Maggie dropped a couple of bright orange bumpers into the water to keep the boats from scraping each other.

Maggie reached over to the bench seat and picked up her red crime scene case, a tool box really, and stepped up on the bench.

Wyatt stood aside and let Axel hand Maggie aboard first, then he grabbed Axel's hand and did the same.

"Hey, Maggie," Axel leaned back against the helm, drinking from an aluminum travel mug. "How's it going?"

Maggie looked over at him and smiled. Axel had always been her favorite among her ex-husband David's friends. They'd grown up together, and if she hadn't loved David since fifth grade, she probably would have gone for Axel, though that would have been a mistake. He was a looker, in that rough, slightly scruffy way that some men were, but he wasn't exactly marriage material, as his two former wives would attest.

"Not much, Axel, what's going on with you?" she asked, setting her case down beside her.

His green eyes squinted under his beanie as he grinned. He pointed at the pile of shrimp with his hand. "We got an extra foot in our last load."

Wyatt and Maggie, both with their hands on their hips, stared down at the pile of several hundred shrimp and one human foot that laid on the deck.

"Well then," Wyatt said after a minute.

Maggie looked at Axel. "Where are the guys?"

"Below," he said, taking off his beanie and running a hand through his brown hair before slapping the hat back on. "Daryl's still discussing the situation with Jesus and I got tired of watching Petey throw up his shredded wheat."

Maggie nodded as she looked at the foot. It was actually most of a calf as well as a foot. Most of the flesh from the calf had been nibbled away by the sea life, leaving just the tibia and fibula bones to represent a former leg. The foot itself, however, was mostly intact. In fact, it still wore a man's Docksider and a brown sock, which, without any flesh to hang onto, had crumpled around the bottom of the ankle. According to the shoe, they had a right foot on their hands.

"Did you guys touch it or anything?" Wyatt asked.

"Well, I tried to roll his sock up for him, but it didn't take."

"You're such an ass," Maggie said, trying not to smile.

Axel nodded in agreement as he lit another cigarette. "Yeah, but my kids seem to like me."

Maggie pulled a pair of blue latex gloves out of her case and started snapping them on. "Is this all that's here? I mean, did you sift through the rest?"

"We kicked it around a little. There's nothing else in there that's not supposed to be."

Maggie reached over and lifted the leg up a little by the end of the fibula. "Well, he wasn't eaten by a shark," she said, lifting the foot a little higher as Wyatt leaned over to look.

"It's been cut," he said.

"Yeah."

Axel whistled around his cigarette. "You sure it's a guy?"

"Yeah, look at the shoe." Maggie turned the leg upside down to look at the sole. "Size 10."

"I haven't seen any missing persons reports come in lately, have you?" Wyatt asked.

Maggie broke her neck looking up at him. "Uh-uh."

"If his DNA's not in CODIS, we might have a little trouble identifying this guy," Wyatt added.

"Yeah," Maggie laid the foot back down.

"If it was me, I'd start lookin' around town for somebody with a peg leg," Axel offered.

Maggie and Wyatt both shot him a look, then Maggie stood up and pulled off her gloves.

"Well, Larry will be here in a few minutes to have a look," she said, referring to the elderly medical examiner. "Dwight's bringing him out."

She looked back toward St. George Island and saw a speedboat off near the tip. "There they are."

She pulled her digital camera out of her case, dropped her gloves on the deck, and handed the camera to Wyatt. "Here, you take better pictures than I do."

"That's because I have an artistic eye," he said.

He squatted down and started taking shots of the foot, while Maggie walked over to Axel.

"Give me a shot of that, would you?"

Axel smiled and handed her the travel mug. She turned it up and took a drink, then choked a bit before swallowing.

"Bourbon, Axel?"

"Hey, this is my happy hour, Maggie. Except I'm not especially happy."

Maggie nodded and looked at the pile of shrimp. "I'm sorry, Axel. You know you're gonna have to throw them all back."

"I don't know why," he answered. "This is my golden hole, Maggie. You know I'll probably catch half of 'em again tomorrow night."

"Yeah, I know. But we won't know that for sure."

"I'll be honest with you, I was within a gnat's ass of throwing that thing over the side. This is a pretty nice haul."

Maggie nodded again as she watched Wyatt get some pictures from the other side of the foot.

"I know. I don't blame you," she said.

A few minutes later, Wyatt helped Larry Wainwright, white-haired and crane-like, board the *Ocean Bounty,* as Deputy Dwight Shultz held his black leather case for him.

"Well, well," Larry said as he peered at the foot over his bifocals. He grabbed Wyatt's hand to hold himself steady as he gingerly knelt down.

They watched him lean in and stare at it up close for a minute.

"What do you think, Larry?" Wyatt asked.

Larry looked over his shoulder and craned his neck to look up at Wyatt.

"Well, it's not a good candidate for reattachment, I can tell you that."

⚓  ⚓  ⚓

*Riptide* will be available in both paperback and e-book in June. You can grab your copy at

# www.dawnleemckenna.com

CPSIA information can be obtained
at www.ICGtesting.com
Printed in the USA
LVOW07s1317311016
511019LV00014B/152/P